CW01020838

WAR OF WITCHES

THE SHIFTER PROPHECY: BOOK 3

MEGAN LINSKI

GRYFYN
PUBLISHING

Copyright © 2017 Gryfyn Publishing

All rights reserved. Printed in the United States of America. No part of this book may be used or reproduced in any manner whatsoever without written permission of the publisher except in the case of brief quotations embodied in critical articles or reviews.

This book is a work of fiction. Names, characters, businesses, organiza- tions, places, events and incidents either are the product of the author's imagination or are used fictitiously. Any resemblance to actual persons, living or dead, events, or locales is entirely coincidental.

Category : Young Adult Paranormal Romance

Summary : Lysandra and Lisar must defeat an army of witches to save both the shifters and the vampires.

For information, contact; **www.meganlinski.com**

Cover design by Molly Phipps

Formatting by Molly Phipps and Megan Linski

Editing by Thalia Smithingell of Gryfyn Publishing

OTHER BOOKS BY MEGAN LINSKI

Alora

These Starcrossed Lives of Ours

The Kingdom Saga

Kingdom From Ashes

Fallen From Ashes

Redemption From Ashes

Prince of Fire

The Rhodi Saga

Rhodi's Light

Rhodi Rising

Rhodi's Lullaby

Creatures of the Lands Series (co-written with Krisen Lison)

Kiatana's Journey by Natalie Erin

Vera's Song by Natalie Erin

Wyntier's Rise by Natalie Erin

Vixen's Fate by Natalie Erin

Midnightstar by Natalie Erin

Angel's Rebellion by Natalie Erin

The Shifter Prophecy

Court of Vampires

Den of Wolves

War of Witches

Heir to Russia

Song of Dragonfire

Song of Smoke and Fire

Change of Wind and Storms

World of Gods and Men

ONE

here are those who believe it's better to have loved and lost than never loved at all.

I despise that phrase. I believe it is better to die than let love slip away.

The moonlight cascades silently upon the Romanian wilderness. I catch a glimpse of Lisar's brown eyes, hiding in the shadows as a wolf. I stoop down in the bushes and motion for him to crouch. Our target, a large deer, is feeding several meters away.

I steady myself. Killing this deer is crucial. Although we're not starving to death, we're running short on the supplies we've cobbled together from hunting and stealing from the local villagers. We need to bring something down soon and preserve the meat so we have something to live on while traveling through Siberia.

After weeks of traveling, we're at the Romanian border. It's now or never.

I focus and compel the deer to come closer. The animal, naturally drawn to the compulsion, begins wandering our way. If I can get it close enough the magic will hold it in place long enough for us to kill it.

Almost there. I wait a few more seconds to take the leap, but Lisar's eyes flash. I hiss, to tell him to stop.

Too late. Lisar jumps too quick and the deer stumbles out of the spell. At seeing Lisar, the deer lets out a bray and takes off.

Lisar bolts after it, his bushy tail waving behind him like a flag. I get up to go after him, and catch up quickly. The deer swings to the side as I run up from behind. Lisar takes a leap to bring the deer down, but the deer delivers a harsh kick to his middle as he's jumping.

Lisar's body flings through the air and smashes against a tree. He groans in pain, curling up on his side.

"Lisar!" I skid to a stop. "Are you okay?"

"Don't mind me. Get the deer!" he grunts.

I whirl around, but too late. I've already lost sight of it. The deer's gone.

I sigh in defeat. Yet another hunt gone bad.

I return to Lisar's side. The wolf shakes his head, then gets to his feet and transforms back into a man.

"Two deer lost in one night. We're losing our touch," he mumbles.

"No kidding." I put my hands on my hips. "Do you think we should keep—"

Lisar grabs my wrist, to stop me. He's completely still. "Listen," he whispers.

I pause. At first, I don't hear anything but the soft tree leaves brushing against each other in the night wind. Then I hear voices. They're far away, but roguish, rough. A bloody smell reaches my nostrils, but it's not one of us. Vampires are in the area. Dragomir's forces.

"We gotta go," Lisar says. He keeps hold of my wrist and starts dragging me through the woods. I glance behind me once or twice, to make sure we're not being followed. Both of us are completely silent, save for our crunching footsteps through the forest terrain.

Only when the bloody smell ceases and the voices have faded away completely do we start talking again.

"That was cutting it a bit short, don't you think?" Lisar asks. He's nervous; I can tell by the way his shoulders are hunched that he wants to change.

"It's not anything new. They've been tracking us for weeks," I argue.

"This is different. They're closer than they were before." Lisar swallows, then licks his lips. "We're going to have to move again."

"Again, Lisar?" I hate that my tone sounds wary, but I can't help it. I don't think we've stayed in the same place for more than a few nights since we left the den.

"We don't have a choice. If we stay where we are, they'll be right on top of us."

Lisar turns to me and grabs my hands. His eyes soften. "You're going to have to back me up on this. The others won't want to move again so soon."

I grasp his hands back. "The Alpha Female always defends her Alpha," I say, and he smiles. An idea crosses my mind, and I add, "Though what if we went back and just took care of them ourselves?"

"What do you mean?" His eyes narrow.

"If I had to guess by the smell, and by the number of voices, there were only four vampires. A small group," I say. "We could go back and eliminate the threat now. Then we wouldn't have to move again and we'd have more time to hunt."

"It would risk exposing where we are," Lisar says. "What if one of them gets away?"

"They won't. I can handle four vampires on my own, and you're an Alpha. We should have no trouble taking them all down together," I say. "It'll give us more leeway to steal the plane. By the time they find the bodies we'll be long gone."

Lisar bites his lip. "I guess it is a good plan." He nods. "All right. Let's do it."

We head back in the direction we came. It seems so silly to return to those we were running from just a few moments before, but after weeks of hiding, I'm tired of cowering in the brush like a little rabbit. I'm a vampire. We aren't meant to hide. We're made to kill.

"You sure this is a good idea?" Lisar whispers to me as we venture closer.

"It's a rational decision," I say. "A good plan."

"You seem to be making a lot of *rational* decisions since you told me you didn't want to marry me."

A flicker of annoyance passes through my chest. Lisar has been going on about his failed proposal ever since I told him no.

"I didn't say *not ever*, Lisar, I said *not right now*," I say tersely. "Would I like to be married to you? Yes, of course. But there's a war going on. People are dying. Do you honestly think it's the best time for a wedding?"

"It's the perfect time for a wedding!" Lisar cries. He swings himself in front of me, flinging his arms wide. "We don't have all the time in the world. Anything could happen to either one of us tomorrow."

"Don't talk like that," I snap. "I won't make a hasty decision just because everything's falling to pieces. If we're going to do this I want to do it *right*, not rush through it because Dragomir's hunting us down."

"I feel like you're making excuses," Lisar grumbles.

"I'm merely trying to be sensible." I swallow. "We would be the first vampire and werewolf to even get married."

"So what's stopping you from making the leap?" Lisar insists. "We're about to make history. Why don't you want to?"

My heart softens at his genuine hope. I cup his face with my hands. "I do want to. Yet there are a million reasons why we shouldn't. We're too young. We're homeless. We're being hunted by our fathers. We have nowhere to go. We don't know if the Siberian coven is going to take us in. Do you want me to list more?"

"None of those reasons are important when it comes down to love," Lisar protests. "And since when have we ever cared why we *shouldn't* do something? Look, Bryn told me you talked to her the night Vasile attacked. I know it's not comfortable for you that we don't know what we are, but I'm willing to put a label on it. Let's just do it. You already know I'd follow you anywhere."

I stroke his cheek with my thumb tenderly. "Bryn was right. Maybe if we were still back at the den, it'd be different, and we'd be planning a wedding right now."

I don't go on to say all the things that would've been different. The den wouldn't be little more than ashes. The Romanian pack wouldn't be scattered across the country, with most of them dead, a few on the run and the rest working for Dragomir. We'd have a home. We'd be safe.

And Lisar's mother would still be alive.

I take a deep breath. "We have to look at the facts. Where do you want to hold a wedding, in the woods? You want to honeymoon in the bushes when no one's watching?"

"That's all right with me." He grins broadly.

I roll my eyes. "Of course. As long as there was alcohol you'd be fine with it."

I lean in to give him a quick kiss. Lisar snickers, and we continue walking. Lisar shrugs and says, "Well, I guess I'll just have to win you over."

"Plenty of women are married to men whom they refused proposals from the first time around," I insist. "You'll just have to wait your turn."

Lisar's face sours at my snarky response. He changes into a wolf and snuffs once in irritation. I repress a giggle and keep onward.

I feel bad for refusing his marriage proposal, but something in my gut is holding me back from saying that three-letter word I desperately want to say. I want to be married to Lisar, but his timing is way off. I just got out of my last engagement with Tomlien a little over six months ago, and Lisar wants me to jump into another one?

No way. I'm taking this slow. I have no doubt Lisar and I will be married eventually, but I'm not going to be pressured into doing something when it's not the right moment, and it's not because I want a big fancy wedding or everything to be perfect before we say I do.

For too long Lisar and I have determined how to run our lives according to how everyone else wants it. From now on I want *us* to decide how things go. I want us to be happy, but on our own timetable.

Not Dragomir's. And that's why I told him no; I need to be sure we're ready, and figure some things out first.

We quiet down as the blood smell reaches our noses once more. It becomes really heavy, almost as strong as the smell of vampires living within Castel de Sange.

Something about this feels off. Four vampires shouldn't be enough to create such a heavy scent. Lisar's eyes catch mine; he's noticed too.

But curiosity drives our pursuit. As we see shadows dancing around a fire, I pin myself against a tree and Lisar spreads out on the ground. I can see them out of the corner of my eye. Their backs are turned.

Lisar mouths *on three*. I nod, and he begins the countdown. When his lips mold *three*, we spring out as one from within the cover of the forest. I unleash my dagger from its hilt on my leg and slash it downward, across a vampire's shoulder blades.

But once the blade hits the vampire, he dissolves into nothing but smoke.

It feels like a freight train has hit my chest. I quickly stab the vampire next to him, but the blade goes straight through his chest. Like the first, he also dissolves right before my very eyes.

"What the—" Lisar sweeps his paw at the vampire he attacked, but it goes right through it, and the tracker disappears. It's as if our opponents were made of air. "What in the hell is going on?"

"They're not real," I say in realization. "They're an illusion."

"What do you mean?" Lisar's still confused, but I'm not.

I sheath the dagger and break into a sprint. "You were right. We need to leave. Now."

"Wait! Lyssy!" Lisar hurtles after me. I don't wait to give an explanation, merely run as fast as I can back in the direction of our camp. Though Lisar can match me stride for stride, even he has trouble keeping up. Fear makes my steps that much quicker, and my breaths that much faster.

I don't stop until we're just outside the camp. I bend over, my hands on my knees, and try to steady myself as Lisar comes screeching to a halt beside me.

"What was all that for? Would you mind telling me what we're running from?" he hisses, panting as he attempts to catch his breath.

"Those vampires weren't real. They were dummies. A spell meant to trick us," I explain quickly.

"I figured that much," Lisar replies. "But what does it mean?"

"It means Valentina is in the area," I say. "She knows we're here. We just walked right into her trap."

TWO

*B*ryn and Tomlien are guarding the entrance to the cave when we arrive.

But I suppose "guarding" is a bit of an exaggeration. They're *supposed* to be guarding it, but really, they're just making out.

"Gross," Lisar says. "Can you guys pry your mouths apart for more than five minutes at a time?"

Bryn and Tom break apart. Bryn puts her hands on her hips, while Tomlien looks cowed. "Lighten up, will you? By Fane. It's not like there's anyone out here."

"Uh, wrong," I say. "There *is* someone out here. We just ran into one of Valentina's spells. She's definitely nearby."

"Valentina?" Tomlien's eyes widen. "That's not good."

"Yeah, no shit," Lisar replies. "So we gotta hustle on down the road."

"We have to leave *again?*" Bryn groans. "But we just got here!"

"Trust me, you don't want to be here when Valentina's around. It's for the best, darling," Tomlien tells her. Bryn lets out an angry growl, while Lisar looks like he's going to throw up at the formal nickname.

I really don't have time to deal with Bryn's pissy attitude right now. I push past her and Tomlien, and Lisar follows me.

In the back of the cave, a small fire burns. Shioni is huddled against a cave wall with Serghei; Kipcha and Rosa are cooking what little bit of food we have left on the fire and Georgie, like usual, is sleeping.

Everyone's in the same spot we left them in hours ago. Weeks living in the wild without showers or ample supplies haven't bothered the wolves much, as they're accustomed to this type of lifestyle, but me and the other vampires definitely don't look good. As for Shioni, the witch appears like death warmed over twice.

"Guys, we gotta go!" Lisar announces as we walk into camp. Georgie gives a snore, and Lisar nudges him harshly with his foot. "Get up, you big loon. There's trouble."

"Wha?" Georgie rolls from his back to his stomach, his large tongue lolling out of his mouth. He changes back into a boy and rubs his eyes before asking, "What's going on, Alpha?"

"Valentina's found us," I say before Lisar can explain. "We ran into one of her spells close by. She's here."

"*What?*" The news causes everyone in the cave to react.

Kipcha comes forward and says, "Lysandra, are you sure?"

"One hundred percent," I confirm. "The spell was hers. It must be."

"Ma... maybe we shouldn't move," Georgie stutters. "What if there are vampires out there? *Not* nice ones?" He gives a quick, adoring glance at me.

"I'd much rather take my chances with a coven of vampires than a witch, especially one as powerful as Valentina," I say.

"Are you sure it's not another witch?" Serghei raises his eyebrow. He's the only one that's remained calm, but I can tell by the haunted expression his face carries that even he's concerned.

"I can find out," Shioni offers. "Witches leave signatures, traces of their magic that can't be separated from their identity. I felt Valentina's signature after I fought her at the den. I'll know if it's her."

Shioni steps out to the head of the cave. She closes her eyes then and her hands, both palms tilted toward the sky.

After a few long moments, Shioni's face darkens and she drops her arms. "Lysandra's right. It is her."

Concerned mutters echo throughout the camp. Kipcha steps up to take charge. "Okay, so that settles it. We steal the plane and leave tonight."

"How do you expect us to steal the plane?" Rosa asks snidely. "We just got here a few days ago."

"We've been watching them," Kipcha counters.

"We've been watching them, yeah, but we don't have a plan," Rosa snipes. "There are humans who work at the airport. How do you know we'll be able to steal one without being seen?"

"Look, nobody is going to be at the airport tonight. It's a small hangar," Lisar snaps. "The humans won't be back until during the day."

When the Alpha speaks, Rosa quiets down. She shrinks down against the floor of the cave at Lisar's glare, and everyone quiets to listen.

"The sun just set a few hours ago. That gives us all night to take it," Lisar says. "But we've only got one shot at this. If we mess up we won't be able to try again, especially not in daylight. The vampires won't be able to move then."

"Not to mention it won't matter, because Valentina will have found us at that point," I sub in.

"Exactly." Lisar nods. He waves a hand. "Pack up your things. We gotta go."

* * *

THE AIRPORT IS SMALL, only ten or so kilometers away. But when we get there we find that instead of it being dark, the entire landing strip is lit up with lights, not to mention the hangar where the planes are kept is heavily guarded. Hope drops when I see the figures of ten or so humans mulling around the hangar.

"There *are* people!" Tomlien shrinks back down in the bushes. "Quite a few of them."

"Told you," Rosa says bitterly. Kipcha biffs her across the side of the head.

"They must be doing mechanical work on the planes tonight. Typical," Lisar mumbles. "Just our luck, huh, Lyssy?"

"We've never needed luck before," I say. I have my hand on my dagger; I'm ready to fight if need be. I won't kill innocents, but I'll injure a few humans if it means getting out of Romania. "What's the plan?"

"If you can get me inside the plane we'll have no trouble," Serghei says. "I'll be able to fire it up in no time."

Lisar's face is scrunched up; I can already guess what he's thinking. "Us wolves will lead the humans off," he says. "The vampires and Shioni will hang back here. Lyssy, wait for my signal. When we've drawn most of the humans away, get Serghei to the plane. Once you've gotten it on the runway, the rest of us will follow."

"Be safe out there," Tomlien says. He extends his arms to give Bryn a hug, moving toward his girlfriend.

"Tom, I'll be fine," Bryn says shortly as she pushes Tomlien away. "There's no need to coddle me."

Tomlien cringes, and pulls away. The rest of us try not to notice.

All of the wolves change. They merge into the night, their dark shadows elongating in the moonlight as they patter down the runway and eventually disappear behind the hangar. I watch Lisar go, only pulling my eyes away from my Alpha when he is out of sight.

Tom's face is long. I can tell he's upset at Bryn's shortness.

"Hey," I say to him. "You wanna talk?"

He doesn't respond, so I go by instinct and walk a short distance away from the group. Tomlien follows, as I figure he would. Serghei and Shioni don't move, but their eyes are on us.

"I'm sorry. I know Bryn's been abrasive since her mother died," I say gently, to start. I avoid using the word *mean* so I don't hurt Tomlien's feelings.

"She's just grieving," Tomlien says somberly. "Though I wish she'd let me comfort her. She keeps pushing me away."

"It seemed like she was letting you comfort her just fine a little while ago." The corners of my mouth twitch.

"It's not the same. All she wants to do is get physical." His face is concerned. "When I try to talk to her, she just changes the subject or starts kissing me again. I don't like it."

"Bryn's a she-wolf, a Daughter of the Alpha. All she knows how to be is strong," I say. "It's hard getting wolves to let their guard down, but you can't force it. You have to let her come to you."

"How can I let her come to me when she keeps pushing me away?" His voice rises.

"Wolves are free, Tom. They're not like us. There's no taming them," I say gently.

"I know." He sighs. "I just wish I could understand what she's going through, but I can't. No one close to me has died. I have nothing to compare it to."

"I know you want to be her knight in shining armor, but grief does some terrible things to people." I stare at the hangar; no signs yet. "You remember how I was. When my mother died I locked myself in my bedroom for weeks."

"I remember." Tomlien looks at me. "Lidia and I tried everything to get you to come out, but when you finally did you told Dragomir you wanted to head to Moscow to train. It's like when you lost your mother, we lost you."

My mouth dries at the mention of my ex-best friend. Lidia. She cared about me back then. Four years was all it took for her to not care for me at all.

"You didn't lose me, Tom, I just had to go do my own thing for awhile," I say. "Let Bryn do hers. It might take some time, but Bryn will come back. She won't ever be the same, but your relationship will be stronger for it. I promise."

Tom says nothing. I decide to let the matter drop. Lisar was inconsolable for a fortnight after Sylvia's death. I knew it best to let him come out of it on his own, and eventually, he did. He's not fully healed, obviously, but the task at hand of getting us all to Siberia safely is enough of a distraction that he's not constantly languishing in his grief.

Lisar might be handling his mother's death better than Bryn, but I don't think that's Bryn's fault. As Alpha, Lisar's instinct to preserve what's left of the pack is overpowering his pain. Bryn doesn't have that luxury.

I can distinguish Lisar's howl from anywhere. When I hear it rising over the treetops, I take it as the signal. "There it is! Let's go!"

I move forward. Tomlien, Serghei and Shioni flank behind me as we run swiftly through the night.

When we get to the hangar, we find it deserted. The wolves did a good job of leading them off.

"Hurry up, Grandfather," I say as Serghei clambers inside the plane, a small utility aircraft. It's not elaborate, but it's enough to fit all of us and carry us all the way there.

Serghei begins firing up the plane. His body moves quickly within the hub of the craft while the three of us keep watch. I grit my teeth and resist covering my ears as the engine roars to life.

The minutes tick by. It feels like we've been waiting at least a half an hour for Serghei to get the plane to run. Small shapes appear in the distance, and they aren't the wolves.

"The humans are coming back! We must leave!" Tomlien hisses. He puts a hand on his sword, but I grab his wrist.

"We aren't going to kill anyone," I say sharply.

Over the sound of the engine is a loud banging sound. We look up; Serghei is pounding on the window, signaling us it's time. Using the ladder, we climb aboard the plane and shut the door behind us just as the aircraft begins rolling out of the hangar.

"We need to pick up some speed if we're going to get this bird in the air," Serghei says as he steers the plane onto the runway. "Where are your wolf friends?"

I spot the pack running like hell at the end of the runway. "There! They're coming!" I point with my finger to show Serghei where they are.

"How exactly are the others supposed to get on?" Tomlien asks.

"Like this," Serghei says. He presses a button, and the loading dock drops out at the back of the plane.

"You've got to be kidding me," Shioni deadpans. She gives Serghei a doubtful look.

"I did it during the war," Serghei counters, as if jumping onto the back of a moving plane is something everyone should be able to do. "Let's see what these wolves are made of."

I walk to the back of the plane. The craft is steadily picking up speed. The wolves have joined us below, but they're already struggling to keep up. They scamper after us on the runway as the plane steadily climbs toward a rate they cannot manage.

There's a rope anchored to the wall swinging near the edge of the platform. I grab it, and tie it around my waist.

"What are you doing?" Tomlien yelps.

"I'm going to help!" I shout back.

Bryn is the closest one to the platform. I extend my arms, and shout, "Bryn, jump!"

She doesn't waste any time. Bryn takes the leap, and I barely manage to catch her. Tomlien darts forward to help me drag her aboard.

"Come on!" Bryn shouts to the rest of the wolves behind her who are still running. "You can do it!"

Rosa is the next to try. She takes a jump, but it's clumsy. I manage to grab her by the tail and save her just before she splatters onto the runway.

"Get off me, you filthy vampire," Rosa snarls, clawing at me.

"You're welcome," I say sharply, then toss her aside.

Georgie is squealing when he leaps. Tomlien manages to catch him by the back of his scruff. The little wolf practically has a heart attack when we pull him up.

I have my arms out for Kipcha, but he doesn't need my help. The beta gives a huge leap and claws his way onto the platform with brute strength.

The only one left is Lisar. He's panting with the effort to keep up with the plane, and he's falling behind. He can't run anymore. He needs to jump, now.

"You need to get a move on!" Serghei shouts from the cockpit. "I need to close the hatch and deploy the wings, or we're going to crash!"

"We're not leaving him behind!" I scream. I lean off of the platform, reaching for him. Lisar jumps…

And misses. I watch in horror as my wolf's eyes widen as he tumbles backwards, off the platform and to certain death.

THREE

"No!" When I see Lisar hurtling through the air, instinct takes over. Time slows down as I sprint off the platform and dive after my wolf. It's an irrational decision, as I don't know if the rope will hold me, but it doesn't matter. Nothing's as important as saving Lisar's life.

The rope catches me around the waist and jerks me backwards just as I latch my arms around Lisar's waist. The air is literally squeezed out of me with the movement, but I don't let go. Lisar changes back into a man in my arms, grasping onto me tightly as we swing back and forth like a pendulum above the runway that races below.

"I don't… have enough strength…" Lisar wheezes. He's tired out from running. All he can do is cling to me.

"Hold on!" I say. With brute force, I start climbing up the rope. I feel a tug on the line and realize that the others are pulling us upward.

The plane's speed races higher, and my hands slip on the rope. Both of us scream as we slide downward, but it's only for a terrifying moment. I force my aching hands to remain fixed on the rope as the platform gets closer and closer.

Finally, we've made it. Lisar and I collapse on the platform of the plane, out of breath. Tomlien and Bryn pull us out of the way as Serghei shuts the door behind us slowly, closing us in.

"Hold on!" Serghei cries. "We're going up!"

The plane jolts backwards at a sharp angle, and Lisar and I go rolling to the back of the plane. Everyone who was on their feet crashes to the floor as Serghei pulls the aircraft up. I suppose he only had enough time to lift off just as Lisar and I made it on. Talk about waiting until the last minute.

Finally, the plane steadies. We're still ascending, but balance is easier to maintain. My ears pop with the altitude gained.

On all fours, Lisar crawls to me. He grabs my face with one hand and kisses me fiercely.

When he pulls away, he's still breathing hard. "Thanks, Lyssy. You just saved my life back there."

"You know I'd do anything for you," I say back. "Even jump off the back of a moving plane."

He gives me a small, loving smile. Serghei's voice bellows over the noise of the plane as he uses the intercom to announce, "Distance from Romania to Salkovia is roughly one thousand, eight hundred kilometers. Estimated arrival time is five a.m."

"What's Salkovia?" Georgie asks curiously.

"It's where we're going," I say. "That's the name of the coven we're traveling to."

"Does it have an airport?" Kipcha asks.

"There's a landing strip about fifty kilometers away from the coven." I swallow. "Hopefully it won't be covered in snow and ice once we get there."

"*Hopefully?*" Bryn snarls. "It's practically winter, Lyss!"

I sigh. "I know. If there was a better way, I'd gladly take it."

"Do you mean to say we'll still have to walk about fifty or so kilometers before we even get there, through the freezing tundra?" Bryn asks.

"Not if we find snowmobiles," I counter.

Bryn gives a dramatic groan. Lisar gets to his feet and stands in front of me protectively. "Look, if there was a better way, we'd take it. But there's not. We're being forced into this."

"No, we're not! We have better options!" Bryn argues. "We have satellite packs in France, America, Africa! We can reach out to them and ask for their help! Lisar, you're the Alpha! If you call out for their aid, they have to answer!"

"The packs are safer where they are," Lisar says firmly. "All of them are still hidden. I'm not going to call all the wolves in the open when our existence is already being threatened. We don't have the numbers, Bryn. There are more vampires than there are us now."

"And whose fault is that?" Rosa clips with a side-glance at me.

Lisar raises his lip, like he's growling, and goes to say something. But to my surprise, Tomlien steps in.

"There is no us and them anymore," Tomlien says. "No such thing as vampires and werewolves. As far as I'm concerned, all there's left are the people who are with Dragomir and those who aren't. And if there aren't that many of us who are against him, it's a better idea to hide those we have while the rest of us figure it out."

Bryn seems absolutely furious that Tomlien disagreed with her. His logic, however, quiets everyone else.

"Guys. I'm sorry that this is happening," I say. "I know you lost your home, your families, everything you've ever known." I steady my voice. "But so have I. We *do* still have each other, and we can't fight. Not now. This is what Dragomir wants. If we keep attacking each other like this, we're going to tear each other apart and then no one will be able to stand up to him."

All eyes are still on me. I try to keep the worry out of my voice as I say, "The vampires of Salkovia aren't friends to Dragomir. He hasn't challenged them yet because they're difficult to get to. Elizaveta will hear us out. She'll understand."

"What's she like?" Kipcha asks curiously.

"Elizaveta's fair. We're very close. She seems cold, and distant, but I suppose you have to be when growing up in the landscape she did. I'm sure she'll help us." I bite my lip. "Hopefully they managed to avoid a similar situation than what happened in Moscow."

"What *did* happen in Moscow, Lyss?" Georgie asks curiously. "You always mention it, but you never talk about it."

The roar of the plane becomes ear-shattering over the painful

19

silence. The wolves look curiously at me, save for Lisar. He's watching me cautiously, a concerned undertone in his brown stare.

I've never spoken about what happened in Moscow. Tomlien and Serghei know, but that's only because they received the news before I came back to Romania. Yet they can't truly *understand*, because they weren't there. I was. I haven't uttered a word about the happenings of that day since they took place.

I haven't even told Lisar.

I shake my head. "It doesn't matter. Just know it was something awful."

Lisar puts a hand on my shoulder. "We should get some sleep, you guys. We have a long journey tomorrow."

Everyone turns away. Rosa, Kipcha and Georgie curl up near the back, while Tomlien lies down on a crate within the cargo hold.

Bryn doesn't try to sleep. She leans her back against the wall of the plane and stares straight ahead with a deadened gaze.

Lisar leads me over to a secluded corner of the plane. He sits me down on a crate before taking his place beside me. We don't say anything, but the moment is loaded with silent words.

"I'm sorry, Lisar." I shake my head as I finally break the silence. "I'm just not ready."

"You don't have to tell me. I don't have to know what happened to realize how badly it affected you," he says softly.

I look down at my feet. "Let's just get some rest," I say. "It'll be difficult getting to Siberia tomorrow. We need to be prepared for anything."

Lisar nods. He knows not to press. He lies down on the crate and I lay next to him. My eyes close almost immediately, yet my dreams are dark, fitful and full of fire and blood.

The plane jolts me awake. It rocks in midair, throwing me off the crate. I slam against the floor, hard, and groan as I push myself upward. Everyone else is awake, too; the turbulence woke them up.

"We've hit a blizzard!" Serghei roars. "Hold on tight!"

The plane wiggles in the air. Everyone grabs onto whatever they can... a crate, the wall, the floor. There's a loud sound, an explosion, and the plane rocks to the side. People scream. The sharp smell of smoke fills the air.

With the sound I'm flung against the wall next to the window, and the plane pitches sharply downward. A pit grows in my stomach, then empties as the plane dives downward like a rollercoaster. Gritting my teeth, I roll over onto the window and look out.

My heart drops when I witness the scene. There's a large hole torn in one of the wings of the plane. It's wrecked.

We're going in for a crash landing.

FOUR

*V*ampires and werewolves can survive devastating car crashes, but I highly doubt that we can live through a plane going down. Yet what can we do? Nothing. The acceleration of the plane hurtling toward the earth is enough to pin me against the wall so I can't move.

"I'm going to try and save it!" Serghei shouts. "Everybody hold on!"

Like there's much else I can do. Lisar is right next to me; our eyes lock. It takes all the strength we have to grab hands. I feel like my hand is going to be crushed under Lisar's tight grip, but I have no doubt I'm gripping onto his just as hard.

I have a view through the window as the ground looms closer and closer... for a minute, I think we're still up in the clouds until I realize what I'm seeing is snow. The plane is leveling out, becoming even with the tundra, but it's not quick enough. It wavers as we hover above ground, then—

CRASH! The sound of metal breaking and twisting apart hurts my ears as the plane touches down, and we're flung to the middle of the plane. My body smashes against the roof, walls and floor, tumbling over and over. I hit a few people as we go, until we're all mushed together in one big heap on the floor. The temperature rises in the plane as the front catches on fire, engulfing the wings in a blazing inferno.

I can't tell if we've stopped. My head is still spinning. There's a rough hand on my shoulder, shaking me awake. My vision fades in and out, ears crowded with white noise. I look up... Lisar... he's shouting at me. Why is he shouting?

Lisar doesn't wait for me to respond to whatever he's saying. He flings me over his shoulder and army-man carries me out of the wreckage.

There's fire, fire everywhere. It blazes red and makes a permanent impression in my eyes. Once again, I hear the cries of Moscow. I dig my fingernails into Lisar's back for a bearing before I lose all strength and the world goes dark.

* * *

It only takes a few moments for me to regain consciousness. The world is cold and hard beneath me; Lisar must've put me down in the snow.

Slowly, I sit up. The plane, a couple hundred meters away, burns brightly under the starry sky. Sunrise, a pink and purple tinge on the horizon, is coming fast.

I look around and count numbers. The panic in my chest eventually lightens when I see that we're all accounted for. We made it. Everybody survived. Serghei managed to save the plane.

Well, I shouldn't say that he saved it. It's completely destroyed. The burning plane is a beacon of light on what is nothing but a plain flatland of white. In all directions, there's nothing but snow and ice. It's nearly enough to drive you mad.

"Lyssy? You okay?" Lisar stoops down beside me and puts a hand on my back.

"I'm fine," I mumble, though my tongue feels thick in my mouth. "I guess we're even now, huh?"

"I'm not keeping track," Lisar says. He stands up again and asks, "Everyone okay?"

There's mottled mumbles of agreement. Kipcha strides up to Serghei and claps him on the back, grinning broadly. "Wow, old man! You weren't kidding when you said you knew how to fly a plane! You really pulled that out of your ass!"

Serghei's lip curls in distaste at Kipcha's crass. "Yes, well, it *is* what I was trained for."

"Lighten up, Grandfather." I hold the sides of my temple. My head is *pounding*.

"We need to put the tents up. It'll be daylight soon," Lisar says. "The vampires need to get out of the sun."

"Did we even manage to save any supplies?" Bryn asks doubtfully.

"I grabbed a few things on my way out of the wreckage," Kipcha says. He gestures to a collection of bags on the ground. "We lost most of it, though. Including the food."

"That's okay. Should be easy to find prey in a frozen wasteland, right?" Bryn says sarcastically.

"Bryn," Lisar says, as a warning. She shuts up, though she gives Lisar a glare.

"We only have one tent, but it's big enough to hold all of us. Should be better anyway. We can huddle together to preserve warmth," Kipcha adds.

"I'm not huddling together with *anyone*," Rosa says, pushing Georgie off of her. He's quivering… the crash really rattled him. I know how he feels.

I get to my feet gingerly and shuffle over to Georgie. I wrap my arms around him and pull him close. "It's okay, little wolf," I say. "We made it, and we're going to be just fine."

Georgie stutters a bit, then quiets down, though he still shakes in my arms.

It's really crowded inside the tent once we get it up. Me and Lisar, as well as Bryn and Tom, don't mind being squished together, but we're the only couples. Kipcha and Rosa are squabbling over space, Georgie won't get off of Shioni, and I can tell Serghei just wants to be left alone. His pride is wounded since we crashed the plane.

The tent isn't made for subzero temperatures, but the wolves' fur makes up for the thin lining. At least it keeps us vampires out of the sun. As it gets lighter, everyone quiets down and falls asleep once more. Lisar's soon out of it, his head resting on my lap.

I don't even try to shut my eyes. I won't be able to rest until we're safely within Salkovia's walls.

Shioni's the only one besides me that's still awake. She shudders against the cold, wrapping her arms around her tightly. She can't bare it as easily as the rest of us. We all made sure to put on our parkas and other winter gear before we embarked on the plane, but unlike us, her body isn't meant to survive extreme temperatures. Georgie, curled up on her lap, is the only one keeping her warm.

"Why don't you cast a spell?" I ask her quietly, as to not disturb the others. "Warm yourself up?"

She shakes her head. Her teeth are chattering. "Can't," she says. "Not enough power."

Something clicks in my head. "We shouldn't have survived that crash," I say. I glance at the witch. "Shioni?"

Shioni shivers, and it's not because of the cold. "I used my magic to put a protective spell around the plane before we landed," she responds. "It gave us just enough time to get out before it exploded, but it drained everything I have. I won't be able to cast a simple spell for at least a few days. Maybe a week, even."

"Most witches wouldn't be able to pull off something like that," I say in surprise. "You should be proud of yourself."

"A witch like Valentina could pull it off no problem," Shioni says snidely. Her nose wrinkles when she speaks of her.

"Valentina's horrid, and she was wrong about you. You're not some weak caster."

"Thank you." A tiny smile graces her face before it slips away. "Though she's right. I am no true Head Witch. Not like her, anyway."

"There's more to you and Valentina than what meets the eye," I say. "Isn't there?"

Shioni nods. "Her coven and mine have a history. I've never met her before she attacked the den, but I've heard stories. She betrayed my family."

"Betrayed you? How?" I ask.

"She stole something from us, a powerful artifact," Shioni explains. "She once was our family's most trusted friend, but we let our guard down and revealed our most precious secret to her. She took it before I was born, to bolster her place in Dragomir's court. My coven died out quickly after."

Shioni sighs. "I am the only one that is left."

"You're still very young. I believe you have the potential to be much more powerful than Valentina," I say. "Don't worry about whatever she took. I'm sure you'll get it back some day."

"Oh, I know I will." Shioni's eyes flash. "That artifact will belong to my coven again even if I have to pry it out of Valentina's cold, dead hands."

I make sure to shut up at that point. I don't want to provoke her further with more talk of Valentina. I like Shioni, but if I've learned one thing over the years, it's that you can't trust witches.

The wolves begin to stir when night falls. We exit the tent, and Kipcha puts it away. I gasp at the beautiful array above. The night is tingling with stars, but there is also a dazzling display of colors, green and blue and purple, that intermingle and dance within the darkness that encompasses the world.

Lisar comes beside me. He wraps my hand in his and holds it tight as we peer upward. "Beautiful, isn't it?" he whispers.

"Yes." I lean against him. "Don't you wish it was just you and me up here?"

Rosa's moans and Georgie's loud complaining about how there's nothing to eat ruin the perfect, contemplative silence. "More than anything," he responds.

Lisar kisses me tenderly on the head. "Come on. We've got to get moving."

Lisar transforms into a wolf. The rest of the pack follows his lead, save for Kipcha, who is carrying the supplies. Serghei takes a compass out of his pocket and examines it, then reads a map.

"If I had to guess we're no more than twenty kilometers from the airstrip," Serghei says. "It should be a quick journey if we hurry."

The group moans, and Lisar and I stay quiet. Serghei, who seems to be the only one who knows where he's going in a world where everything looks the same, pivots in one direction and heads forward. The rest of us follow him.

As the hours tick by, stomachs grumble. What's left of our dried meat is passed around the group. The wolves are better suited to the environment, but just grumpy because they're hungry. The cold doesn't bother me, but my throat is dry and burning from a lack of blood. It's painful, but not enough to deter me. Tomlien's eyes are bloodshot, and Serghei's steps have slowed… I can tell both of them are thirsty as well. I can't wait to get to Salkovia and chug a bottle of blood.

Shioni's steps are rigid, like she's going to shatter into a million pieces with each step. Miniature icicles hang off her eyelashes I'm scared she's going to freeze to death before we get there.

Lisar is the only one who isn't complaining. He stares up at sky that's lit up by the beauty of the northern lights, his eyes glimmering. Sometimes he runs far ahead, his gaze toward the sky. He's chasing the moon, his tail a flag behind him as the arctic chill ruffles through his gorgeous sandy fur.

I leave the mopey group behind and venture forward to join him. His entire form seems to glow against the shimmering, perfect snow.

"You love it up here, don't you?" I ask. I feel like I'm creating something for us, a pocket tucked away against the world that others can't fracture or ruin.

"Yes. I'm happy up here." Lisar glances at me. "Despite the bitter cold, this is a place I feel I could stay."

"What do you like so much about it?" I ask.

He doesn't take long to answer. "No responsibility."

I nod. "I understand."

And I do. Here in Siberia, you could run forever. Nothing changes. The land stays the same, and so, life does as well. Very few people live up here. There is no one to rule over, no decisions to make and no consequences if you choose the wrong path.

Lisar and I *could* stay up here. Overall, that's my plan. Bryn might want to rally the others to fight, but no one has told her that our purpose in coming here wasn't to fight at all. It was simply to get away.

We can't fight Dragomir. It's a fool's hope to resist him. The only option is to run. As far as I know, Dragomir has no interest in coming to a land of ice and snow. His ambitions don't go this far north. He'll spend years in Romania looking for me, but I won't be there. I'll be safe. We'll be safe. Lisar and I can start over.

And maybe then, we can get married. Like we want.

The night is much longer than the day here in Siberia this time of year, which gives us more time to travel. In the distance, I see several snow-capped mountains… hope. We're nearly there.

The group breathes a collective sigh of relief when they see a small hangar floating in the distance upon the snow. It looks abandoned; there aren't even any planes here.

"Is this place even used anymore?" Kipcha asks as we venture closer.

"There are snowmobiles that they keep around the back," I say. "If we're lucky, they'll be there."

I've been here before; this is the airstrip I took when I first came to Salkovia. We used the snowmobiles to get there after the plane dropped us off.

I navigate the group around the hangar. The snowmobiles are indeed there, but something else is lying in wait for us.

A coy, red-lipped smile is the first thing I see, accompanied by a red velvet cloak that clashes like blood against the white snow. Five other lone figures, hooded in black, make a singular line behind her.

The witch removes her hood with long, manicured fingers. Her dark eyes sparkle with a terrifying glee as they fall upon me.

"Hello, Lysandra," Valentina says. "What took you so long to get here?"

FIVE

*H*orror wraps its long, clammy fingers around my middle and squeezes. Nobody moves; we're as frozen as the tundra that surrounds us.

Another figure, this one cloaked in black, steps out from behind Valentina. I recognize her smug smirk before her eyes meet mine.

Lidia. I haven't seen her since I left the castle. A bubble of hatred wells up inside me, but I stuff it down. I'm not interested in revenge. My duty is to keep Lisar and the rest of us safe. Right now, escape is the first priority.

"Really, Lysandra, you should've known better." Valentina *tsk tsks.* "Salkovia? It's too predictable to know where you'd run to."

"I think I should've known better to kill you when I had the chance, but I won't make that mistake again," I snarl.

Valentina laughs cruelly. "We can't all be gifted with intelligence, dear. Unfortunately, you won't live to regret it."

Valentina sends a bolt of purple magic hurtling my way. Lisar screams, but Bryn is the one closest to me.

"Lyss, get down!" she screams. Bryn slams her shoulder into me, tackling me to the side.

But she can't get out of the way fast enough. The bolt meant for me slams into her, and volts of purple electricity run across her body. As if electrocuted, Bryn's eyes roll in the back of her head as she falls onto the snow with heavy convulsions.

"How sad," Valentina says dryly as Bryn curls up on the snow. "That really was meant for you."

"Bryn!" Tomlien shouts. He runs to her, and falls to his knees at her side. He glares at Valentina, murderous rage upon his face. "What did you do to her?"

"Nothing she didn't deserve," Lidia responds coldly. I refuse to acknowledge her; how could she have become so different? Or was she always this way, and I never wanted to see it?

"Enough senseless chattering," Valentina says. "Lysandra, I'm here to escort you back to your father. Will you come quietly, or must we do so by force?"

"You can forget it, lady," Lisar growls, and he launches himself at Valentina. Valentina waves her hand, and Lisar is thrown harshly against the side of a snowmobile.

His attack causes everyone to spur into action. Kipcha, Rosa, and Georgie all take a witch. Tomlein gets up and screams. He pulls out his pistol and fires it at Valentina, releasing five shots. The bullets hit an invisible shield in front of Valentina and drop away, like he never did anything.

Serghei moves in on Valentina. He pulls out his *shahska* and slinks toward the witch silently in a surprise attack. But without seeing, Valentina knows he's coming. She ripples her fingers and Serghei drops his weapon, doubling over in pain.

"Grandfather!" I rush to him, but someone gets in my way... Lidia.

It doesn't take me but two seconds to whip out my dagger. I point it at her as a warning and say, "Back off. You know better than to get in my way."

She narrows her eyebrows at me and says, "Aw, how cute. You honestly think you can take me and my magic?"

"You can't be a witch," I say scathingly. "You don't have any magical blood. I would be able to smell it running through your veins. You're just a weak human."

"I was *always* training to be a witch, Lysandra," Lidia hisses. "But you were too busy making out with your dog to notice."

I lose my temper. I raise my dagger and charge at her with a crazed yell, but she puts up the palm of her hand. As she does so, I'm blasted backwards.

The wind's knocked out of me as I collapse on the ground. I sit up in utter shock. She cast a spell. But she shouldn't be able to do that. It's impossible for a human to have magic.

Something isn't right.

"Impressed, Lysandra?" Lidia gives an obnoxious cackle. "I always loved imagining the look on your face when I finally knocked you on your ass. It's even better than I fantasized."

"Don't plan on seeing it again," I growl. I use the balls of my feet to push myself upwards and launch at her again. I swing the dagger upward, but Lidia counters me with another spell, this time an invisible shield like Valentina's. I swing and jab at her from every angle, but even when my aim is true my blade stops inches before it makes contact with skin.

Lidia dances out of the way of my hits, her fingers curled together to hold up her shield. I'm pleased to see that she can only do defensive work. She's not as powerful as Valentina. Hell, she's not even half as powerful as Shioni. But I still can't break through her defenses.

I use all my strength on the next blow. There's a cracking sound, like glass shattering, and for a moment I almost manage to nick her skin. But Lidia twists her hands and my feet are knocked out from underneath me.

"You forget how many hours I wasted watching you practice," Lidia hisses as I clamber upright once again. "How you fight's like a rerun, Lysandra. You only know how to do it one way."

The sound of an engine roaring to life diverts my attention. Lisar's on the back of a snowmobile, Bryn draped limply over his lap.

"Everyone get to the snowmobiles!" Lisar roars. His eyes connect with mine, telling me to run, before the snowmobile shoots forward and races off to safety.

I don't waste any time. While Lidia's snarling at Lisar, I take the chance to smack her across the face. My nails draw blood, and she screams as she tumbles to the snowy earth. I start running in the direction of the snowmobiles.

There are two dead witches, their bodies nothing more than piles of ash on the ground by the wolves' feet. Georgie's been immobilized by a spell; Rosie grabs him by the collar and drags him to a snowmobile, where she changes back into a girl. She drapes him over her lap like Lisar did Bryn before taking off. Kipcha ties the supplies to the back of his own snowmobile before following.

Tomlien's already on the back of a snowmobile. I leap on behind him and wrap my arms around his waist.

"Hold on! I'm gonna push this thing to its limit!" Tomlien screams.

"Tom, wait! What about Grandfather?" I shriek, looking over my shoulder.

Serghei is still bent over in pain. His mouth is open in a horrifying, silent scream, face contorted into a visage of pain. Valentina doesn't notice her dead companions… she only wears a look of extreme satisfaction as she watches Serghei be tortured by her spell.

I'm about to leap off the snowmobile and help before someone else intercedes. Shioni strides up behind Valentina, then taps on her shoulder.

Valentina turns around, her defenses down. Shioni literally *punches her in the face*, then grabs Serghei and drags him over to a snowmobile of their own.

It doesn't take them but a few seconds to clamber on and be off. Valentina cradles her face, screaming in rage.

"Time to go," Tomlien says, and he fires up the mobile. I'm jerked backwards when the snowmobile jumps forward. I squeeze Tom's middle tightly (which, by the way, isn't half as firm as Lisar's abs) as the snowmobile builds speed and catches up to the others.

I look behind me, expecting Valentina to pursue, but she doesn't. She merely stands there and watches, becoming a dot on the horizon that disappears from view.

Out of everything that's happened today, that frightens me more than anything.

Lisar waves his hand to us, and Tom pulls ahead of the other snowmobiles.

"You're going to have to tell me where to go," Tom shouts to me. "I don't know the way."

"Head north," I tell him. "It's pretty much a straight shot from here."

Tomlien turns the snowmobile slightly, and off we go. The freezing cold claws at my face as we race the mobiles across the open plain. Each moment seems longer than the last, the darkness lengthening along the earth. All that exists is the sound of the engine, and the bitter cold, which creeps over me like an impending doom.

Eventually, the snowmobiles slow down and run out of gas. We're forced to clamber off of them ten kilometers outside Salkovia.

Or, at least what I can guess is ten kilometers. It can't be much farther away.

"Is everyone okay?" Lisar asks as he hops off his snowmobile. I look around at the others. Georgie is unparalyzed, and Serghei has recovered from the torture spell. Bryn is still unconscious; she hangs over the seat like deadweight, though she's still breathing. Her back moves up and down in low, steady movements.

"I think we're all right, save for Bryn," Kipcha says, looking at her in concern. "We don't know what happened to her."

Everyone glances at Bryn worryingly. Tom slides off his snowmobile, and ventures over to her with long, cautious strides.

"Careful," Lisar warns anxiously. "Valentina said that spell was meant for Lyssy. We have no idea what that means."

Tom's ignoring Lisar's words. His gaze is focused on Bryn.

"This isn't right," Tomlien says. His voice rattles with fear as he approaches Bryn. "Valentina had the advantage. She could've easily overpowered us, but she let us go. Why did she let us go?"

Tomlien reaches out a hand. He places it lovingly on Bryn's back, and that's when she startles awake.

Bryn looks up at Tomlien. At first, her gaze is confused, murky. Like she just woke up from a strange dream.

Then, her eyes darken into two pools of rage, fear... and hatred.

"Bryn? Are you all right?" Tomlien asks.

Bryn wrinkles her nose, and her face twists into a painful grimace. With Tom's hand still on her back, Bryn gives a loud growl. Without warning she changes into a she-wolf, and leaps snarling for his throat.

SIX

*T*omlien reels backward. By instinct, he grabs Bryn around the shoulders to hold her back.

Bryn has become a crazed, wild animal. Her mouth foams as she snaps her mouth several times by Tom's neck, eyes bloodshot and wide. Her claws scrabble at Tomlien's face as she attempts to rip out the eyes.

Tom screams in pain as her nails cut into his skin, but he doesn't let go. His arms shake with the effort of keeping Bryn off of him. Slowly, he begins to squeeze, to cut off her air supply. Though her breaths are ragged and raspy, she doesn't stop the pursuit of taking his life. Only becomes more violent.

She doesn't care that he's hurting her. She just wants to kill him.

"Bryn!" Lisar launches forward and wraps his arms around Bryn's middle, trying to pull her off. Bryn doesn't bother with her brother, nor realize that he's got her. She only scrabbles to get to Tomlien, her insane gaze still fixed on his horrified stare. Unable to hold his balance, Lisar tumbles backward onto the snow, taking Bryn with him. He twists and turns as Bryn struggles to get back to Tom. She digs her paws into the snow and inches forward, jaws salivating.

"Hold her down!" Lisar shouts. The pack members all rush to help. Kipcha, Georgie, and Rosa collapse on top of Bryn. Bryn squirms under the hands of her packmates, growling and snapping. It's literally taking all four wolves to stop her.

Eventually, Bryn slows. Her breathing calms. Her eyes lose that crazed look, and foam ceases to leak from her mouth. She settles. Reluctantly, the pack releases her.

Lisar is the last to let her go. He's still got a firm hand on Bryn's shoulder when she transforms back.

The girl shakes her hair of out her face. On her knees, she looks up at Tomlien.

"What… what just happened to me?" she asks, her voice weak.

Tomlien's hand is around his throat, where Bryn's teeth nearly were. He grips the seat of the snowmobile tightly as he leans against it. His face is full of pain, immense hurt. He looks like he's going to cry as he stares at Bryn with a look of utter betrayal.

"Tommy?" Bryn whispers. "Tommy, baby, what did I do to you?"

He doesn't say. Bryn looks to me for answers. Her gaze is pleading and lost, like a dog who doesn't realize it's been abandoned. I just realize that I've watched the entire scene without doing a damn thing. I was frozen the entire time.

"Shioni. Do you know what sorcery is among us?" Serghei is level-headed enough to break the silence; his strong voice is the only one of reason.

Shioni clears her throat. "It is a cruel trick. One of Valentina's harshest. She cast a spell that would render the receiver unable to stand being touched by their lover. If they even brushed by her skin, the receiver would go berserk and attempt to murder her beloved."

"So that means if Tommy touches me again, I'll try to kill him?" Bryn asks. Her voice wobbles. Tears are running quickly down her face. "I won't be able to touch him ever again, forever?"

"Not forever," Shioni says quietly. "Only until the caster of the spell passes away."

Bryn's head drops. Tomlien's hand removes from his throat, but it's still shaking. An awful pit of guilt forms in my stomach.

Valentina cast that spell for me. She wanted me to be unable to touch Lisar without trying to kill him. She was trying to get us to murder each other, to stop the resistence against Dragomir.

What a cruel, hideous fate. Being unable to touch the man you love? Why, that's nearly enough to make a relationship fall apart. What a terrible, sick trick to play.

Yet Bryn took it for me. And now my friend has to suffer the consequences.

"That's why she let us get away," Lisar says. "She thought that once Bryn went crazy we'd all take sides and turn on each other. That way she wouldn't have to do the job."

"She never did like getting her hands dirty," Serghei says nastily. The contempt for Valentina in his voice is enough to make me reel. Not even during the worst parts of the war did he speak of an enemy in such a way, but I suppose this is much more than just a war. This is personal.

Bryn and Tomlien are avoiding each other's eyes. I can tell it's killing Tomlien not to be able to comfort Bryn when she cries.

Lisar finally lets go of Bryn's shoulder, and stands. "It's okay, Bryn. We'll get rid of the witch. That'll break the curse."

"How are you going to do that? Valentina's practically unstoppable!" Bryn shouts. Her sobs increase in intensity and sound. Seeing a strong she-wolf like her break down like this is enough to make me cave inwardly. Bryn doesn't break. She gets angry, heads into battle with a vengeance, rages against the world. She doesn't give up.

"It doesn't matter," Lisar says softly. "Just believe we will, all right?"

Bryn sniffs loudly. She wipes her face with the back of her hand. She gets up to sit on Lisar's snowmobile, opposite Tomlien. They seem so far away right now. The sight of one friend crying and the other miserable is enough to make me sick.

"We played right into her trap. She knows me," I whisper hatefully. "She *knows* my first instinct would be to go to Salkovia. How could I be so blind?"

"It's not your fault, Lyssy," Lisar says quietly. I can sense he wants to embrace me, but doing so would be a low blow to Bryn and Tom right now. "It's not like we had options."

"This doesn't make any sense," Kipcha says. "Valentina found out we were at the Romanian border not soon before we got on the plane. How could she have gotten to the base before us?"

We all look to Shioni, but she gives no answer.

That only terrifies me more. At least with words, you have something. But with silence, there is no hope. Only desperation, and a terrible fear, because you don't know what's coming next.

Another thought crosses my mind. Something troublesome. "There's something else," I start. "Lidia and I fought. I tried to hurt her, but I couldn't. She has magic, and I don't understand how. She's human. Witches are born, not made."

I give a side glance to Shioni. "You have to have magical blood in order to be a witch. Don't you?"

Shioni hesitates. "There *is* a way. But it's incredibly rare."

"How? Tell me." I move closer.

Shioni nibbles at her lip. "Lidia would've had to sell her soul. Essentially, give herself up to Valentina. Any command she gave, Lidia could not disobey."

My veins turn cold with shock. An image appears in my head… one of Lidia signing a contract, and then Valentina extending her hands, dark magic stemming from within them and wrapping their icy tendrils around her my former friend's form.

Lidia, twisted over in pain. Lidia, crying out in a terrible, tortured scream. Falling on the floor and begging for mercy, for the pain to end.

Then the pain stops. Lidia rises to her full height with a manic smile on her face, drunk on magic and mad with power.

Just like Dragomir.

"So Lidia is drawing from Valentina's power, and not her own?" Tomlien's question jolts me out of my thoughts.

"Basically. Valentina is so powerful, I doubt she'd notice any magic missing from within her." Shioni's teeth draw blood on her lip; I can smell it in the air. "Yet that's what worries me. Lidia could grow to be a supremely strong witch under Valentina's discipline. To have *two* witches like her running around…"

"It'd basically be a disaster for us," Lisar finishes.

"So we solve this problem the same way we solve Bryn's. Kill Valentina," Georgie offers, a bit too optimistically.

"You make it sound so easy. Valentina's more difficult to kill than anyone, even Dragomir," I say. "Any wound you could deal her she could heal, any trap you could lay, her magic would protect her from."

"It would have to be a witch who did it. Someone who cast a murder spell," Shioni whispers quietly. "It's the only way."

"Could you do it, Shioni?" Bryn's voice rattles with an edge of hope. "Could you kill Valentina?"

Shioni stands perfectly still as she looks at Bryn. I know the answer to that question. I can read it on Shioni's face.

But it's too much for this handmaiden to say to her princess, someone she dearly loves.

Shioni shakes her head. "I don't know. Maybe."

Bryn's hopeful gaze slides away. A freezing cold wind brushes by, permeating the bones of all in the group. Lisar shivers, and says, "Let's get a move on. Dawn isn't too far off."

"We're nearly there," I add, to encourage them. "Let's go."

We leave the snowmobiles behind and begin the trudge through the tundra. It's a pretty quiet walk.

Eventually, electrical lights appear on the horizon. The closer we venture to them, the more my mind eases. Salkovia. We made it.

The wall surrounding the village is large, and very tall. Made of stone, the structure rises up four stories. The only way into the coven is through two giant wooden gates directly in front of us.

To my immense surprise, the gates open when we venture near them. Kipcha goes to walk through, but I throw out a hand to stop him.

"Hold on," I say. "Something's not—"

They come from the dark. Hooded figures cloaked in black drop down from above, falling off the wall and onto the snow. They land one by one, then form a circle around us, a tight band we cannot escape. I swallow nervously as our group huddles together. The Salkovian vampires are known for dramatics.

A tall, slim figure is the last to fall. She lands directly before me before rising up and casting back her hood.

Her white hair is tied back in a braid, blue eyes flashing. Her high cheekbones accentuate a thin nose and almond eyes. She draws herself upward proudly, holding perfect posture. Everything about her is distinctly Russian. And very dangerous.

"Elizaveta." I sigh in relief. I long to embrace her, but now is not the time. "I'm so grateful we found you."

"Why have you led wolves to our door?" Elizaveta shows no warmth, not at the moment. Her cold eyes, chilling as the Siberian landscape, observe the pack suspiciously. "You know you are always welcome here, but they are not. Why have you arrived with our enemies?"

"We have nowhere else to go," I say. "We come seeking sanctuary. Dragomir seeks our lives. Mainly, my life."

"For what?" Elizaveta's eyebrow raises.

I'm proud I don't stutter. "For loving a wolf. You must know."

Elizaveta's lips become pursed. "We've heard stories. But I had hoped the rumors weren't true." She eyes Lisar. "This is the one, isn't he?"

"Yes." I gesture to him. "The Alpha."

"Hm. Well." She shrugs. "You could've done worse."

Kipcha snickers, and Lisar punches his leg. Elizaveta's attention goes to Kipcha. When their gazes connect, something very strange happens. Kipcha's eyes dilate, and Elizaveta becomes very still. The moment is very fragile, breakable like glass. It's almost like the two of them are the only ones there.

I know exactly what's going on, because it's happened to me. My mouth opens, but I have the sense to close it before anyone sees.

Elizaveta finally rips her focus away from the wolf, and nods at me. "Very well. I can understand the difficult situation you're in. Though I'm not sure what I can do about it."

"It's easy. Let us in," I beg. "We won't cause any trouble. We're merely seeking peace."

"This is preposterous!" Another vampire steps forward. He's older, nearly Serghei's age. "You want us to allow you into our village? The vampires, fine, but the wolves among you cannot be let in! They're different from us! They cannot be trusted!"

"They are the last of their pack," Serghei argues. "They are not a threat."

"Serghei, I served under you, and have the utmost respect for your position," the vampire responds. "But you're asking the impossible. Will the Salkovian vampires allow wolves to live within our ranks? Possibly. But to stand up to Dragomir by allowing you asylum? You'd have to be half mad!"

"To be frank, half of us are already mad," another vampire mumbles. "You have to be, to live in Salkovia."

A few of the members within the circle chuckle, but most stay silent. Elizaveta sweeps her cloak behind her. "The others are right. We are no friends to Dragomir, however, his forces overpower ours. If he discovers you have hidden yourselves among us, which he no doubt will if he hasn't already, he will come here to wage war."

"Won't you defend us?" I plead. "Will you not fight him if he comes?"

"We wouldn't fight for refugees," Elizaveta says. "But for our csarnia? Anything."

A chill enters my stomach. They're not looking to hide us. They want a leader, someone to gather the rebels together, a poster child to stand against Dragomir. A champion against an impossible cause, and, if things go wrong, a scapegoat to blame that isn't one of their own. But that's the exact opposite of what I'm trying to do! I'm trying to hide from Dragomir, not raise up a banner against him! How could these vampires ask such a thing of me?

It doesn't matter. I have no choice.

"You want me to become your csarina? Fine." I cross my arms. "What must I do to gain your trust?"

"Prove yourself," Elizaveta says. "We shall set forth a trial for you to pass. If you succeed, you will become our csarina, and we will be devoted to you."

"And if she doesn't?" Lisar steps forward to stand at my side. "What if she doesn't pass?"

Elizaveta turns slowly to him. "If she should fail, she will not survive the task, and we will have no choice but to cast the rest of you out. Lysandra will be dead, and you will have nowhere else to go."

SEVEN

I don't even have to think about it. "Deal. Now let us in."

"Uh-uh. No deal." Lisar steps in front of me. "Lyssy, we can go somewhere else," he whispers in my ear, putting a hand on my elbow. "This isn't necessary."

"You forget I trained here. Whatever they have to throw at me, I can handle." I pull away from Lisar's grasp slowly and look at Elizaveta. "Take me to the trial."

Elizaveta nods. She turns. Her cloak sweeps behind her as she strides through the open gates. The rest of the Salkovian council presses in around us, and we follow Elizaveta as she begins the venture through town.

Salkovia has always been a beautiful village. The cobblestone streets, lightly dusted with snow, shimmer under streetlamps lit with candles. The buildings are made of bricks, each of them topped with cupolas or onion-shaped domes. The structures are colorful, painted bright reds, soft whites, luscious blues and calming pinks, with doors made of bronze. The walls are thick, the windows small and narrow.

The feeling of the village is very classical, every house styled in Russian Revival architecture. The snowflakes drifting softly from the puffy clouds above make the town look like a Russian Christmas card.

The cathedral, easily the largest building in town besides the

House of Antov, shines in the rising dawn with roofs made of gold. I've seen it all before, but Salkovia's charm never ceases to wrap me within its spell.

Just before the sun rises Elizaveta leads us into a large square building with a rounded roof. I know this place well. It's the stadium in which I used to train. Inside is a large dirt arena, surrounded by metal boards with plastic windows and stands that rise up to the ceiling.

She guides us to the locker rooms, where she opens a locker and takes out a black mass of clothing with a pair of combat boots.

"My uniform," I say as she presses it into my hands. I'm surprised she still has it.

"Did you think I'd get rid of your things? Never," she says with a grim smile. "Change, and enter the arena. Your trial will begin soon after."

Elizaveta sweeps out the door. When the door claps shut behind her, Serghei is the first to move forward. He cups my chin with his hand firmly as he says, "Stay light on your feet. Don't try to overpower them; you won't be able to handle two at once. Your best bet is your agility. Take them down quickly, before they see what's coming."

"I will, Grandfather. You have nothing to worry about." I kiss him lightly on the cheek.

"I will be watching nearby with the rest of your... companions." Serghei eyes the wolves as he pulls back. "We will be waiting for you at the gates when you succeed."

Serghei exits the locker room. The rest of them mutter goodbyes as they follow his lead.

"Good luck, Lysandra," Tomlien utters. He reaches out to take Bryn's hand, before he thankfully remembers and skirts away. Bryn follows him, eyes down. She doesn't say a word.

Only when we're alone in the locker room does Lisar begin worrying. "*Two of them?*" he asks. "What exactly does that mean?"

"Maybe you shouldn't watch," I say. His eyes are on me as I strip of my clothes and pull on the uniform, a black unisex bodysuit made with mesh fabric. I lace up the combat boots before standing upright. "It's only going to freak you out."

"Lyssy, I can't let you do this." He starts forward and grasps me tightly. "There has to be another way."

"We have nowhere else to go," I say firmly. "Valentina's out there. If we leave Salkovia she'll catch us in a minute. The only reason she can't get to us here is because there are hundreds of vampires in her way."

Lisar doesn't seem convinced. I take a deep breath and add, "I can do this, Lisar. I promise."

His expression is sullen. "If I get any idea that you're going to get killed out there, I'll break down the damn wall and save you."

"I know." Before he can say another word, I lean forward and kiss him. I can taste the saltiness of his mouth as our lips touch. Lisar opens his mouth, and our tongues intermingle in a passionate dance. I wrap my arms around his waist, and his large hands encompass my hips tenderly as we finish the kiss.

Lisar pulls away and puts his forehead against mine. "Please don't die."

"I won't." I untangle myself from his arms, though it's painfully difficult. I'm glad I enjoyed that kiss. It might be the last kiss I ever get.

We leave the locker room and venture toward the arena. The benches surrounding the arena are filled with vampires, hundreds of them. I guess good news travels fast.

A roar at the end of the complex gets his attention. Lisar's head whips around. He makes a strangled, choking noise as he sees two gigantic male polar bears wandering free in the dirt area, bellowing at each other.

Lisar's face is completely white. "Polar bears?" he asks. "You have to fight *polar bears?*"

"I've killed polar bears before during training," I say. "I mean, it was only one polar bear, and it was hard, but if I can handle one then two should be no problem, right?"

Lisar looks like he's going to pass out. Kipcha wanders up from behind him. I'm grateful for his presence right now; he'll need to drag Lisar away.

Kipcha glances at Elizaveta, who is standing at the doors of the arena, in awe. "They use *polar bears* to train vampires? Who are these crazy bastards?"

"Lyssy," Lisar squeaks. His eyes are terrified.

"I'll be fine, Lisar. I love you," I say finally, before I give a pointed look at Kipcha. Kipcha wraps his arms underneath Lisar's armpits and starts hauling him backwards, toward the stands. I feel bad for Lisar; he not only has to fight against his own feelings, but instinct to let me go in alone. Bonding isn't easy.

"I've told you before I disagree with your environmental standards," I say to Elizaveta as I approach the doors. "Polar bears are endangered, you know."

"We breed our own stock. This is our way," Elizaveta responds solemnly. "It has been a tradition for hundreds of years, even before we became vampires, for the people of Salkovia to slay polar bears to prove they were worthy of leadership. There is no better way to earn the respect of our village."

"Yeah, well," I say, taking a deep breath. "When I'm csarina there are gonna be some updates."

I stride forward before she can make another comment. I'll save the earth later. The doors to the arena close shut behind me, locking me in.

The second I'm inside, the attention of the polar bears is on me. They were going to fight each other, but at the scent of my vampire blood they immediately consider me the greater threat. They gamble toward me at full speed, roaring and snarling.

I don't move. I'm too busy making a plan.

I killed my first polar bear by stabbing it in the back of the neck. That won't work this time, as I don't have a weapon. I have to kill them with my bare hands.

The larger one reaches me first. He rears up on his hind legs to slash at me with his large claws. I roll out of the way just as the second skids in front of me. He lashes out with his large teeth, but I manage to spin out of the way.

My punches are strong enough to crack bone. While I'm by the smaller bear's leg, I reach backwards, then deliver a sharp blow with my fist. I hear the tell-tale crack of the bone breaking, and the bear moans in pain.

I jump away, satisfied I've slowed one, but I was so busy focusing on him I didn't pay any attention to the other bear. He grabs my thigh in his mouth and lifts me off the ground, shaking me.

The crowd screams and gasps. His teeth sink deep into my leg, penetrating through to nearly the bone. The agony is nearly blinding. I cry out in immense pain before forcing myself to curl upward and smacking the bear harshly on the nose.

The bear flings me across the arena. I go flying through the air and slam harshly into the boards. They shake with the impact. I moan, and turn over on my side to observe my injuries. The bear punctured several holes in my leg with its teeth, making the fight even. I can't run. I can barely walk.

The bears are already racing toward me again. I struggle to stand, and wince as I put weight on my injured leg. It's going to be painful to fight like this, but I've dealt with worse things than pain.

Tears stream down my face as I launch myself out of the way of the stampeding bears. The injured one slams into the boards. He collapses against them, stunned. The other spins around. He rears on his hind legs again and pulls back his paw.

This time, I'm not quick enough. The crowd gasps the same time the tips of the polar bear's claws connect with my side.

I gasp, and instantly put a hand to my middle. I pull it back to see that it's gushing blood.

But I got lucky. A few more inches and he would've gutted me.

The bear goes to come down upon me, but I grab its paws and hold it back, wrestling with the bear. The bear's jaws snap inches from my own face.

Out of the corner of my eye, I see that the other bear is getting up.

Groaning, I use all of my strength to literally pick up the bear and toss him across the arena and into the other bear.

It achieves what I wanted it to. Angry, the polar bear that was thrown turns on the one it landed upon. The polar bear pins down its injured companion and begins mauling it, ripping out its throat and innards.

When the bear is dead, the victor steps away and turns back toward me, roaring its fury.

One down. One to go.

Lifting a polar bear is no easy feat, even for a vampire. I'm exhausted and injured, but I still have one left to kill.

My vision goes in and out as the bear charges. I don't have that much time left. I'm going to faint at any moment, then the bear will have a feast. This needs to end.

Stay agile, Serghei whispers in my head. I remain still.

The moment the polar bear lunges at me with its teeth, I swing to the side, feet planted on the same spot. I wrap my arms around its neck just as its mouth misses my torso.

"Sorry," I whisper. Then I snap the polar bear's neck.

The light dies in the polar bear's eyes. I let its heavy head fall from my arms as the beast collapses onto the arena floor, dead.

I waver back and forth on my feet. Just as the crowd begins to cheer, I pass out.

* * *

LIGHTS ARE above me when I awaken. I sit up slowly to find that my uniform has been replaced by a flowing, long-sleeved nightgown. I can tell by how rigid my middle is that my wounds have been bandaged. My leg is also stiff, wrapped tightly.

I've been placed in my old room in the House of Antov. It's a beautiful room, with a four-poster bed and a lovely armoire. It must mean that they've agreed I've proved myself. Some would argue that a csarina should have nicer quarters, but here in Siberia, this is the best they have.

The door opens. I'm relieved to see Lisar enter. He's carrying a large bottle of blood.

"Hey there," he says. He sits on the bed and hands the bottle to me. "You need to drink this. No option."

"Gladly." I uncap the bottle and start chugging. Relief floods into my body as I drain the blood from the container.

I only stop when I can drink no more. The bottle is only a quarter full. As I put it down on the side table, I can feel the injuries underneath the bandages knitting. By the time I'm done with that bottle, I'll be completely healed and at full strength again.

"Remind me never to make you mad," he says as I wipe my mouth. "You were a total boss out there."

"I'm a good fighter," I say. "But I guess I took a few hits."

"That's putting it lightly." Lisar unties the top of my gown, and looks downward. He grimaces as he observes the injuries.

"Hey, no peeking," I tease.

"Yeah, okay, because that's what I'm doing." Lisar shakes his head, then reties the gown. "Like sex would be fun anyway with you all banged up."

"I'll be fine by the time morning rolls around. You'll see." I grab the bottle and take another sip of blood. I'm so thirsty.

The door clicks. To my displeasure, Kipcha, Tomlien, Bryn, and Elizaveta enter. I really wanted to be left alone with Lisar for a moment. We haven't gotten much time together since we left the den, but I guess politics can't wait.

"How you doing, Lyss?" Kipcha asks.

"Probably better than Lisar." I groan as I shift on the bed, and give a mischievous glance at my wolf, who doesn't seem amused. "I imagine he wasn't very complacent when the polar bear was attempting to pull my leg off."

"Uh, he about killed me trying to get to you," Kipcha said. "It took all of us to hold him down."

"*All* of us," Tomlien confirms. "Wolves, vampires, everybody." He glances at Bryn in the corner. "Well, almost."

Bryn doesn't say anything. It's like she's become mute ever since she's been cursed.

Serghei walks in, holding a clear bottle of Russian vodka. He's drinking it straight out of the bottle, no chaser. He takes a long drink before standing at my bedside.

"Grandfather, shouldn't you be drinking blood?" I ask, raising an eyebrow.

"I assure you, Lysandra, I need this much more." Serghei takes another swig. I don't know how he can do that without his eyes and throat burning. It's practically blood to him.

Elizaveta steps forward and says, "The council has discussed, and we've decided to follow you. We acknowledge you, Lysandra Romanova-Dracula, as csarina, and deny Dragomir's claim to the throne. We will offer you asylum and agree to house your wolves, so long as they make no attempt on the lives of our people."

"Thank you, Elizaveta," I say. "I sincerely appreciate it."

"I suppose the question is what you want us to do now." Elizaveta crosses her arms. "You know word of this will reach Dragomir. We must have a plan to stop him."

I hesitate as she gazes at me expectedly. Everyone is looking to me for an answer, except Lisar, who shifts next to me uncomfortably.

I let the silence linger too long. "You don't have a plan?" Elizaveta's eyes are wide as she asks the question.

"Not yet. I was merely concerned about getting here, about survival. I have no strategies to go up against Dragomir. Not yet," I add hastily.

Elizaveta shakes her head. "Very well, Lysandra. We will wait for you to come up with something. But you know that the Salkovians *do* expect you to have a strategy to protect us, correct? It's your duty as csarina."

I nod. Elizaveta stares at me before she leaves the room. Her gaze appears very worried.

"She's right, Lysandra," Serghei says lowly. "You are csarina of Salkovia now. They expect you to lead."

"I know." I sigh heavily. Serghei opens his mouth to say more, but Lisar stops him.

"Okay, everybody out," Lisar says. He stands up and starts pushing people toward the door. "Lyssy needs to rest."

Lisar locks the door behind them when we're finally alone again. He sits beside me just before I start crying. It's not a full breakdown, but I'm still pretty upset, though I feel my tears are more out of exhaustion than anything.

"I didn't come up here to lead anyone," I say. I lean against Lisar's shoulder. He wraps an arm around me and holds me close. "I just wanted to get away."

"I know, Lyssy." He wipes the tears from my face with his thumb. "I didn't want this, either."

"I don't want to make a plan against Dragomir. I don't want to go to war. I just want to hide." I can't help how weak and helpless I feel right now, and I just took down two polar bears. All this stress is getting to me.

"It's going to be okay, Lyssy," Lisar says soothingly. "I promise. I'll do whatever I can to make this right."

Lisar lets me cry in silence for awhile. He doesn't say anything, just holds me, which is what I need more than ever right now.

Finally, I stop crying. I wipe my face and pull away from his embrace. "Let's just get some sleep," I say. "It's been a long night. Maybe things will be better tomorrow."

"Of course they will. I'll be there to make it better."

He kisses me tenderly before walking to the vanity to pour himself a cup of water from the glass jug sitting upon it. I take another sip of blood as he does so.

Lisar begins to drink. But as he lifts the cup to his lips to take a sip, it drops out of his hand. The glass tumbles through the air, smashes on the hardwood and sends water spilling across the floor.

"Lisar!" I scream. I get up from the bed and rush to him. Foam is leaking from his mouth. His face turns red, eyes bloodshot and bulging. He puts a hand around his throat as he gasps for air, seemingly unable to breathe.

The answer clicks in my head as he makes the gesture. He's been poisoned.

"Lisar," I whisper. I go to grab him, but I'm too late. Lisar reaches out for me as he collapses onto the floor.

His eyes lock with mine just before they close. He twitches once, then lies still.

EIGHT

I start screaming. My knees skid on the floor as I fall beside Lisar. I grab his shoulders and start shaking him. "Lisar, babe, wake up, please wake up…"

No matter how hard I shake him, he doesn't awaken. I give a choked sob and put two fingers to his wrist. A wave of relief crashes over me when I feel he still has a pulse, though it's faint.

His breaths are light, ragged and gasping. With no other ideas, I pick him up in my arms and carry him out of the room, crying out for help.

"Help me! Someone, please!" I shout. "Lisar is dying!"

Vampires begin emerging from their rooms. Serghei, who is bleary eyed, immediately sobers when he notices my limp wolf in my arms.

"What happened?" he demands.

"Lisar got a drink, then he started foaming at the mouth like he was choking, then he just collapsed!" My words come out blubbering and jilted. "I don't know what to do!"

"Give him to me." Serghei takes Lisar from my arms, turns around and starts carrying him in the other direction.

"Would you all mind your own business?" he barks at the vampires peering curiously at us. Subdued, they return to their quarters.

Serghei leads me through the hallways and to a lone door at the end of the house. He nods to it. "Go ahead and knock, Lysandra."

I bang on it, *loudly*. Shioni opens the door, her hair a mess and wearing silk pajamas.

"What's going on *now?*" she asks when she sees Lisar. Foam is starting to leak from his mouth again.

I quickly explain as we enter. My mouth drops open when I see what's inside. Besides the bed the room is filled with vials, bottles, cauldrons, and potions of all sorts. A strange brew bubbles in one of the cauldrons near Shioni's bed.

This is a witch's lab, reserved for the Head Witch of Salkovia. Why is Shioni in here? Maybe the Head Witch moved to a different room.

Serghei carefully lays Lisar down on a cot in a corner of the room. Shioni stands over him, pressing a finger to her chin in thought.

I worry over Lisar as Shioni presses her hands into his shoulders. She closes her eyes, and her brow furrows as she concentrates.

When she pulls her hands away, her expression isn't one I find comforting. "It can't be," she whispers.

"What?" I yelp. "What's wrong with him?"

"Shioni!" Bryn practically breaks the door when she enters. It makes a loud, slamming sound against the wall, which I'm sure wakes the whole house. "You've got to come quickly, there's—"

Her words break off when she sees Lisar lying immobile on the cot. "What's wrong with my brother!?"

"Probably the same thing that's happening to the other wolves, if I had to guess," Shioni says grimly.

"The other wolves? What are you talking about? We just work you up!" I shriek.

"Take me to them, Bryn." Shioni is rolling up her sleeves. She goes to follow her friend, but I grab her pajamas and jerk her back.

"What about Lisar?" I ask.

"He'll be fine. I promise he's not going anywhere," Shioni says. "Where are they, Bryn?"

"I left them with Tommy. I don't know what's wrong, they were all eating, and then…"

Bryn's voice fades away as she leads Shioni away. Serghei glances at me before rushing out to follow.

I start pacing the area by Lisar's bedside nervously. He seems to be getting better, and the color is returning to his face, but he's still sick. Where is Shioni, and why did she leave us here?

It isn't a but a few minutes later that they return. Serghei is carrying Kipcha, Bryn's dragging Rosa, and Tomlien's got Georgie. Each of the wolves are similar to Lisar… foaming at the mouth, unconscious, barely breathing.

This is a horror story straight out of a nightmare. Someone's been poisoning the wolves. Bryn's the only one that hasn't been affected.

Tomlien arrives, accompanied by Elizaveta. She's still in her cloak. Does she ever sleep? She maneuvers around Shioni as the witch observes Georgie, putting her hands on his shoulders just like she did with Lisar.

"Elizaveta, why is Shioni in here?" I whisper to her. "Isn't this where your Head Witch stays? Can't she help with this?"

"Our witch left," Elizaveta explains. She presses her back against the wall. "Two weeks ago."

"Left?" I ask, astonished. "Why would she leave?"

"I'll explain later." Her eyes remain fixed on Kipcha as Shioni looks at him, then moves onto Rosa.

Finally, Shioni pulls away. "It is just as I feared. All of them are affected by the same spell."

"Spell?" I ask, confused. "What do you mean?"

"Valentina. She poisoned the water supply with a potion of hers," Shioni says grimly.

"If that is so, shouldn't all of us be sick?" Serghei asks.

"The potion doesn't have any affect vampires or witches. Just wolves." She shakes her head.

"Then why wasn't I affected? I drank the water, too," Bryn argues.

"You can't be cursed twice. The more powerful curse will rule out the other," Shioni informs her. "When you took the spell for Lysandra, it made you immune to the potion within the water. You can't be hurt by it no matter how much you drink."

"So what's wrong with them?" I ask, still scared.

"You'll see." Shioni folds her arms around herself. "They should be waking up any moment now."

As if on cue, Lisar's eyelids flutter open. I start forward. My arm wraps around his shoulders to help him sit up. He seems dazed, and sways back and forth once he's finally upright.

"What happened?" he asks.

"You fainted," I say.

"Ugh." He puts his hand over his eyes. "I feel like I'm gonna be sick."

I reach for a nearby cauldron and put it under his head. He dips his head inside and gags a few times, but he doesn't vomit.

Slowly, he pulls his head out of the cauldron and looks at me.

But it's not the same look he alwasys gives me. It's like he's staring right through me, as if I'm not even here.

Something has changed in his brown stare. But I don't know what it is.

"Do you feel any different?" I ask.

"No…" Lisar shakes his head groggily, then his eyes contract. "Wait. Yes."

"What do you mean?" I ask quickly.

"No!" Georgie's yelps of panic catch my attention. I whip my head over my shoulder to see that he's fallen out of his cot, and is floundering around the floor in a panic. "Alpha, I can't change!"

"I can't either," Rosa stutters. She's shivering all over, like her body is consumed by a bone-chilling cold.

"Help me, Alpha!" Georgie's cries for Lisar increase in intensity as he scrambles to get to his feet. He smashes several vials and knocks aside cauldrons as he stumbles, nearly drunkenly, around the room. "Help me!"

"Lisar…" Kipcha groans his Alpha's name desperately as he winces in pain, getting off the cot. I've never seen the beta like this. Not when he was being tortured by Dragomir. Not when the den was on fire. But now, he's terrified.

"Oh god, no." Lisar bends over, his hands tangled within his hair. "No, please no…"

Words from the past break into my head, a terrible promise uttered by the witch herself. *"For years, I've been working on a spell to defeat the shifters, and I finally have perfected it. One drop of this potion will render a shifter unable to change. I will quickly be able to replicate the spell. Soon, we will have the capability to use this upon all the wolves, and defeat them once and for all."*

Valentina's potion. The one she created with Lisar's blood. She finally made another potion, and used it. She's finally rendered the wolves unable to change.

Lisar is pleading with Fane for it not to be true. Kipcha and Rosa watch him mournfully, while Georgie scampers around the room.

The sight is sickening.

"I can't change! I can't do anything!" Georgie cries. He trips over his own feet and smashes into a cabinet, knocking a few bottles askew. "I'm a wolf! What am I going to do if I can't *be* a wolf?"

"Georgie, cut it out!" Lisar snaps. He gets up from the cot, lunges forward and snags the boy by the shoulder. He holds him tight, and stares into his eyes. "Stop."

Georgie calms down, though he's still shaking all over. Lisar lets him go. Georgie teeters over to the other side of the room, to sit in a corner quietly.

"How did this happen?" Lisar whirls on me. "Tell me."

"Valentina. She poisoned the water supply with a potion she made," I say quietly. "I'm guessing you can figure out which one."

Lisar's eyes widen. He runs a hand through his hair again, momentarily speechless. Bryn steps in to take his place.

"It's probably part of a bigger plan to poison the satellite packs," Bryn says. "She and Dragomir already wiped out most of us. This just seals the deal."

"She can't poison them if she doesn't know where they are," Lisar says. "We were just the guinea pigs."

"Please, tell us you can fix this." I step toward Shioni. "There must be a way."

Shioni sighs. "I don't know. I'll need a blood sample from all of you, and one from Bryn, to test it against. I need to study what she's done. There might be a way to reverse this. But I don't have the answers right now."

The wolves drop their heads, hopeless. Elizaveta, who has been like a statue, finally moves. She goes to the center of the room, her loud voice commanding attention. "Valentina knows you're here, that much is obvious. But this isn't the first move she's made against Salkovia. Her forces have been attacking us for weeks now."

"Her forces?" Serghei's gruff voice deepens. "You surely mean Dragomir's forces."

"No." Elizaveta shakes her head. "Her own. Our Head Witch left to join her shortly before you got here."

"What are you *talking* about?" Tomlien asks. He's angry… his fists are bunched up tightly, mouth tight. I don't blame him. Both of our wolves now are suffering as a result of this war.

"In the past month Valentina has created an army of witches to eliminate the covens that oppose Dragomir," Elizaveta says harshly. "Those who agree to align themselves with her will receive benefits. Money, power. Even a country. After the warring covens have been eliminated the witches will be given a kingdom of their very own."

"Something that witches have never had before," Shioni says. Her eyes are wide.

"Dragomir obviously promised Valentina something incredible," I say sourly.

"Obviously." Lisar kicks a wayward cauldron across the room. "I guarantee that he agreed to let Valentina be the queen of this witch kingdom once she gets done doing his dirty work."

"We have been able to keep them at bay, so far." Elizaveta sighs. "But it won't be for long. The only reason Valentina hasn't targeted us more effectively is because we played impartial. We did not acknowledge Dragomir as our csar, but neither did we oppose him."

Elizaveta's eyes flicker to me. "That ended today when we proclaimed you csarina."

Guilt wiggles through my stomach. I play with a wayward strand of hair and say, "Fine. Then we kill Valentina, and end her witch army. We have to fight."

"How can we fight?" Kipcha gets up off the cot. He grabs a cauldron and starts squeezing it. I can smell the blood that pools out from his hands as he presses his fingers against the strong metal. If he was still a wolf, he would've crushed it easily, but no longer. The potion renders all of his wolf powers useless, making him just as weak as a human. "How can we do *anything* when we can't transform?"

"We're just going to have to make it work," Lisar says quietly. "We don't have a choice, Kip."

I give Lisar an affectionate gaze. How can he still support me after what I've done to him? His love is miraculous.

Shioni stands over the cauldron that was bubbling earlier. She peers into the concoction, a thick, blue substance. She passes her hand over the potion and says, "It doesn't matter. Kipcha is right, the wolves must be able to defend themselves. But this curse has a time limit."

"What do you mean?" Lisar asks quickly. It sounds like someone is drawing a noose around his neck as he says the words.

Shioni doesn't look at him. Her eyes are absorbed by the sight of the potion. "The spell will only be reversible for so long. If I don't find a cure soon, you and the other wolves will be stuck this way. Permanently."

NINE

I find Lisar sitting on the ledge of a large water fountain in the greenhouse a few hours later, his head buried in his hands. Elizaveta pulled me away almost immediately after Shioni told me us bad news. She wanted me to talk with her council, which I didn't care for. I don't give a damn about Salkovia's defenses right now; I just want to comfort Lisar.

I didn't have a choice. If Valentina had the ability to poison our water system, she knows our weaknesses and can get in anywhere else. The title of csarnia carries a heavy burden, made heavier by the fact that I don't know what I'm doing. All I was able to suggest to the council was to heavily fortify our defenses, increase the guards protecting the walls, and install a plan of retaliation if Valentina decides to attack. We don't make a move, but wait for her to come to us.

All common sense. I don't know why they expect me to have some grand plan to defeat her. I can barely keep myself straight. My heart just isn't in it.

The greenhouse is attached to the main hall. It is the only way that the vampires can grow plants here to eat, as supplies can't be shipped here easily. An array of vegetables, alongside flowers, stand in neat rows in tables that line the walls.

The fountain is beautiful, and large. Two marble lovers entwined in an embrace stand at the top of the fountain, water flowing out from their feet in a fan.

I pause for a minute to observe my wolf. I've never seen him so broken. He seems lost. Incomplete somehow, like only half of him is there, and the other half has been stolen away.

I sit beside him. He doesn't move.

After a minute or two, I chance to say something. "Seems so odd, doesn't it," I comment. "A world full of green in a place where it only snows."

Lisar doesn't respond. He merely moves so his head is leaning against my arm. I press into him.

"I can't feel my bond to you." Lisar's voice is aching. "It's not there anymore. I still love you, but it's not pressing on me like before. I used to be unable to stand it when you were away."

He sighs. "I can't change. I'm not strong anymore. I can't see in the dark. I can't even smell. Not like I used to."

He raises his head. His eyes are red-rimmed. "I'm not *me*."

"I know it feels like that, but you *are* you," I insist. "You haven't changed."

"Yes I have."

"Lisar." I grab his face with my hands. "We *will* find a way. I won't leave you like this. I don't care what Shioni says. There is a way to break this curse. I will go to the ends of the earth to find it."

"You can't. Not as csarina." Singular tears fly off his face as he shakes his head. "You have too much responsibility on your shoulders to worry about me."

"I already told you this war can go to hell. I don't care about them, I care about us."

"You made *promises* to these people, Lyssy. You agreed to protect them if they took you in." Lisar takes a deep gasp. "You can't go back on that."

He's right. But I don't want him to be.

"I just want you to be okay." I press his head into my chest, to

64

muffle his cries so the rest of the house doesn't hear. "I swear to you Lisar, I will do whatever it takes to make this right."

* * *

DAYS PASS. Shioni works tirelessly, day and night, to seek a cure for the curse that afflicts the wolves. I visit her every day to see how she's doing, but it's always the same answer. No progress yet.

Most of my day is taken up by stupid responsibilities that I don't want, such as endless council meetings, talking politics with strangers and overseeing the defenses around the city. Serghei has thankfully taken it upon himself to manage the army and train the vampires for whatever's coming, which relieves a burden from me, though it still weighs at the back of my mind.

But not even my duties as csarina are as crushing as the pain I feel when I think of the wolves. Rosa keeps herself locked up in her room, and Georgie has taken to following around whoever can tolerate him at the time like a lost puppy.

Although not afflicted by the curse, Bryn is just as grumpy as the rest of the pack, if not even more so. I don't know where she goes; she vanishes for long periods of time. I'm nearly certain she slips out of Salkovia to go hunting on a daily basis, as she can't change around here without one of the other wolves bursting into tears. Her leaving is dangerous, as Valentina's forces could spot her, but I stall on confronting her about it. I can't handle her temper on top of everything else right now.

Tomlien avoids her by helping Serghei. To say they're not getting along is an understatement. Bryn's inability to touch Tomlien, or even be around him without beoming extremely irritated, is driving a wedge between them. I've gotten tired of listening to her and Tom fight day and night about things. It's almost a relief that she's gone, another reason why I haven't said anything to her.

Kipcha is the only one who seems interested in actually living. He spends most of his time with Elizaveta, who has taken a liking to him. She gives him things to do, like making sure the armory is adequately stocked and helping her fortify the wall. It's like he's her new personal helper.

I'm glad he's keeping busy. Though he's still unhappy about the effects of the curse, he's doing well and moving forward.

Lisar, however, is not. He keeps staring out the window. That's what he does all day… just sits there and stares, from the moment the sun sets until it rises once again in the morning and it's time to go to sleep. I've tried dragging him along to some of my meetings just so he has something to do, but when we're there, he doesn't move. He doesn't talk, he barely eats… it's like I'm living with a ghost, a specter that has just chosen to fade away.

I'm extremely worried about him.

It's been a fortnight since we arrived in Salkovia, and Lisar hasn't left the house since the night we got here. I figure I must do something to cheer him up. He hated being locked up in my room at Castel de Sange. I can't imagine that he's any happier here hiding away in the House of Antov.

"Lisar," I say, to get his attention. We've just finished dinner, after a long day of me consulting with people and Lisar… being odd. The moon is full, creating a brightly lit night. I put away the dishes on a rolling tray the cook brought us. Lisar barely touched his food.

"Babe, let's go do something," I say. I roll the cart into the hallway and close the door behind me. "I want to get out of here before they come looking for me. Do you want to take a stroll downtown? It's a nice night. I haven't shown you around Salkovia yet."

He doesn't respond. I feel like I'm talking to myself. I stride before him, bend down, and look him in the eyes. It's like they're completely dead.

"Hey. *Wake up.*" I grab his shoulders and shake him. "Come on, let's go."

Lisar finally moves. His fingers are loose in mine as I drag him upward. He plods slowly after me as we wander through the walls of the house, and even slower once we get outside. It's absolutely freezing, but it's not snowing.

"There's the blood factory," I say as we pass it. "And the residential area, and the shops. It's not a big town, you see. There are only a few hundred or so vampires who live up here. They get their blood from the local wildlife, and from farming. They actually bottle their own. It's quite spectacular."

Lisar remains quiet. Feeling rather like a tour guide, I stuff down my frustration and say nothing.

"What's that?" Lisar asks. I jump at the sound of his voice, which I haven't heard in days. His finger points toward an old wooden bridge that connects two sides of Salkovia, a large ravine underneath.

"That's Sorrow Bridge," I say. "Peculiar name, I know," I say when he raises his eyebrow. "They call it that because Salkovia was actually two towns, once. The rumor goes people on opposite sides used to fall in love with each other, but they couldn't be together because the divide was too wide."

I kick a snowball and send it skittering. "I suppose they didn't realize the situation was as easily solvable as building a bridge."

"It doesn't look very safe," he comments.

"It's falling apart. I'm surprised they still let vampires use it," I say. "It wouldn't take much for it to collapse."

"But you'd survive the fall," Lisar says.

I shake my head. "Unlikely. It's a long drop, and there's a river that runs beneath. The top is frozen through several inches thick. Even one of my kind would plummet to their death."

The Salkovians ignore us as we pass by, like we're any normal couple. The only good thing about this curse is that the vampires of Salkovia seem more willing to tolerate the wolves living among them, as they don't pose a threat. It's a step forward in the direction of peace.

My semi-good mood is ruined when I see Elizaveta coming up the walkway, Kipcha on her heels. I raise a hand in greeting, though I want to strangle her with it. Can't I get just one night alone to spend with my boyfriend?

"Hi guys," Lisar says dully when we come together on the path. "What are you up to?"

"I was looking for Lysandra. I need to talk with her," Elizaveta says. "Just for a moment," she adds quickly when I frown.

"It's fine. I was actually going to ask Lisar if he wanted to come with me to the bar," Kipcha says, jerking a thumb in the opposite direction. "You don't mind, do you, Lyss?"

"Of course not," I say, too brightly and too quickly. Lisar glances at me and I say, "You guys need to have fun. Go ahead. Elizaveta and I will join you later."

"Lyssy…" Lisar says. I can tell by the look on his face he's searching for an excuse to get out of it. Okay, if Lisar doesn't want to have a drink, I *know* something's really wrong with him. Time to fix it.

"Go!" I shove him toward Kipcha. It was meant to be playful, but it's obvious I'm trying too hard. "Enjoy yourself."

Lisar stumbles forward, and Kipcha catches him. My boyfriend glances over his shoulder helplessly at me as he's dragged away by his best friend. I give him a muddy smile back. Not too promising. But if I can't get him out of this stupor, maybe Kipcha can.

"I'm sorry to disturb the two of you, but we have pressing matters at hand," Elizaveta informs me quickly. "I sent Kipcha to take Lisar away because neither of them can help and I don't want the Alpha overhearing. We've found the army of witches. They've made camp not ten kilometers away."

"So what do you want me to do about it?" I ask, a bit too crassly.

"I expect you to do *something*." Elizaveta crosses her arms. "They're right where we want them. I know you said you didn't want to make a move, but this is the perfect opportunity. We should strike before they do."

Ten kilometers away. That really is nothing. Valentina wouldn't be so close if she didn't think she was going to attack soon. It's right out in the open, with nowhere to hide.

"All right," I tell her. "When the sun rises, wait for me in the training arena. I know what we have to do."

"What's your plan?" Elizaveta asks anxiously.

I put my hands on my hips. "We're going on a special ops mission. Before the day's over, I'm going to kill Valentina."

TEN

*A*s planned, Elizaveta meets me in the training arena as the new day dawns. Shioni has come with me; I requested her presence, as we'll need her help to kill Valentina. She's got the sun lotion. She was able to whip some up quickly once I told her our plan. Elizaveta and I smear it on our skin before heading out into daylight.

Lisar is still out with Kipcha, which is promising. He won't notice I'm not in bed and come looking for me.

The streets of Salkovia are empty as we slip through the streets. All the vampires are in bed. Elizaveta opens the large wooden doors without any problem, and just like that, we're past the wall.

Three snowmobiles lie in wait for us outside. We board them, and follow Elizaveta as she leads the way to the encampment across the tundra.

This is the best way to solve things. I kill Valentina, then Bryn's curse is undone and Salkovia won't have to worry about an army of witches attacking us at any moment. Without a leader, the group of casters will dissolve and go elsewhere. Then we can focus strictly on finding a cure, and getting the wolves back to normal.

Valentina's immensely powerful, but only when she's awake. She can't protect herself when she's sleeping, not unless she put protective charms around herself, which is why we brought Shioni. She'll disable the charms, I'll move in, and we'll slit the witch's throat before she can wake up.

Easy.

Two kilometers before we reach the camp we leave the snowmobiles behind, so the witches don't hear us coming. As we near the camp, Shioni maneuvers between us.

"Don't you think this is a bit obvious?" Shioni asks. "Valentina is too clever to leave her army right outside Salkovia."

I open my mouth to respond, but before I can, a brown shape comes sliding down an embankment of snow right at me. It hits my legs and knocks me over. I go bowling into the snow.

"Ouch!" I hiss. My hip landed right on a patch of ice. I glance up and see that Bryn was the one that fell into me, after losing her footing on the embankment. "Are you kidding me? What are you doing this far out? You shouldn't be out here!"

"Neither should you!" Bryn snaps. Her tail curls behind her and her ears flatten back. "Why are you here?"

"Why else? We're going to kill Valentina," I reply sharply. "You've obviously seen the camp if you've been running around out here."

"Camp?" She tilts her head, confused.

"Yes, *camp.* Valentina's army is out here. We're going to sneak inside and kill her before she can attack Salkovia," I say. Why is she being so annoying right now? Just get with the program, Bryn!

"Lyss, I've been coming out here for days. There's no camp, and if there is, there's something off about it." She shakes her head. "A whole army can't just spring up overnight."

"Our scouts saw it last night. It's not more than a half a kilometer to the south." Elizaveta points.

"Did it pop out of the snow?" Bryn asks sarcastically before shaking her head. "No! Think!"

"You're being overly cautious. Don't you want a shot at her?" I ask. "You can end your curse and be with Tom again! Don't you want that?"

"Of course I want to be with Tommy!" Bryn's eyes flash with hurt when she says his name. "But don't you think if I noticed Valentina was here I already would've tried to end her? I'm telling you, Lyss, this is a trap!"

I take a deep, steadying breath. "Trap or not, we're going through with it if it means getting a shot at Valentina," I snap. "Now either fall in line, or get out of the way!"

Bryn utters a low growl at me before reluctantly joining Shioni's side. The rest of the walk is made in silence, though it's a heavy one.

Emotion runs thick throughout the group. It doesn't bode well for us. We won't be able to keep our heads straight during a fight, but we have to do this now. We can't wait for our window to pass.

Finally, we come to the campsite. There are far fewer tents then I thought there would be, clustered around in the snow.

The camp is quiet. All the witches are obviously sleeping. There's no movement inside.

"It's like a ghost town," Shioni comments. Her eyes are narrow as she surveys the camp.

"I thought you said there were hundreds of witches with Valentina," I say, glancing at Elizaveta.

She shakes her head. "It was an estimate. If this is all there are, we should be grateful."

I nod, and remove my dagger from its holster on my leg. "You're right. Let's go."

The three girls trail behind me as we enter the camp. We're so silent, not even our feet crunch upon the snow. We don't want to take the chance of waking anyone else up. We wind and bend through the tents, searching for Valentina but not quite sure where she could be.

Finally, we find the biggest tent in the middle of the camp. A banner with the sign of my father's house flies outside, red and proud against the wind.

"That's gotta be it," I whisper. I motion for the others to come near. They venture closer, and we move as one unit behind a collection of tents.

I jerk my head toward Shioni. She raises her hands to survey the protective charms around the tent. Her face becomes a mottled jumble of confusion seconds later.

"There are no spells surrounding the tent." Shioni drops her hands in disbelief. "It can't be. Something about this isn't right."

Anxiety twists in my stomach. Valentina wouldn't leave herself unprotected. I take a deep breath, walk forward, and suppress the urge to yank back the flap of the tent. Slowly, I peel it back so we can step inside.

Inside, we don't find Valentina. But we do find Lidia. She's curled up on a cot underneath some blankets, her face nestled in the pillow. She appears peaceful and dreamy. Nothing like the horrible person I know she can be.

"I'm going to keep watch," Shioni hushes. She slips back outside, and Elizaveta follows her. Bryn and I are the only ones left inside the tent with Lidia.

"Kill her, Lyss," Bryn whispers. "Have it over with."

I swallow. My mouth has become very dry. I move toward the cot until I'm standing directly over Lidia. I grip the knife tightly in my hand. Sweat is coating the hilt. If I had a heart, it would be pounding loudly. I can't breathe.

Looking at Lidia now, it's hard to imagine that she betrayed me. She seems so young and innocent, just like she did when she used to sleep over in my room. There doesn't seem anything menacing about her. Did she really mean to hurt me, or did she just get caught up in jealousy? Perhaps she regrets what she did. If I forgave her, would she come back? Could we learn to love each other again?

I lower the knife so its almost against her throat. The sight of my hand pending to take her life makes me nauseous. This was my best friend. Can I really kill her in cold blood?

"What are you waiting for?" Bryn moans. "Do it!"

I can't. Just as I'm going to put the knife away, Lidia's eyes snap open.

The innocent expression vanishes to be replaced by a cunning smile. "I knew it. You're so easy to fool."

"Lysandra!" Shioni's cry comes from outside. "The other tents are empty! We have to run!"

I can't believe I was so stupid! I bring down the knife, but Lidia grabs my wrist and twists it. A sharp gasp of pain escapes my lips, and I'm forced to drop the knife. I try to yank away, but I can't. With Valentina's power, Lidia's just as strong as I am.

Bryn springs to tear out Lidia's throat, but Lidia knocks her aside and rises to her feet. She clamps down on my wrist, and I scream in pain as her touch becomes burning hot, like an iron is being pressed onto my skin.

Bryn growls again. Lidia's hit didn't even phase her... she's too caught up in revenge. While Lidia is focused on me Bryn leaps up and grabs Lidia's arm. The wolf bites down. Lidia lets me go and starts screaming bloody murder as she tries to rip her arm away from Bryn's mouth. No matter how many times she punches Bryn on the head, she won't let go.

"Bryn, we've gotta move!" I reach for my dagger, switching it to the left hand. I'm just as good with this one as I am the other. Bryn lets go, and Lidia falls to the floor. She cradles her mangled arm as the two of us escape.

I skid to a stop the second I'm outside. The tents. They're all gone. Not a trace of them remains, save for the one behind us.

Then it hits me. It was an illusion. A trick. The army was never here.

Bryn was right. I fell right into Valentina's trap.

Six witches, each cloaked in dark black, surround us on all sides. Their hoods fall in front of their eyes so we can't see their faces. We have no choice but to fight.

Bryn is the first to make a move. She flings herself on a witch and goes for the face. The witch blasts her off with a shot of blue magic, but it doesn't even bother Bryn. The she-wolf gets up and goes right back on the attack, this time aiming for the legs.

Shioni wastes no time. She begins dueling with two witches at once, shooting jets of magic of every color at her foes. Both dance out of the way, casting spells back at her just as fast as she can come up with them. Neither can best the other. All are too equally matched. The most the rest of us can do is get out of the way.

I brought my pistol just in case. I grit my teeth as I fire the gun against the burning pain in my wrist. The bullets hit one witch, but not another. The bullets merely ping off of her and scatter everywhere as she advances toward me in slow, steady steps.

She goes to grab me. I smack her over the head with the butt of the pistol. The witch crumples to the ground, unconscious. I duck as a spell from Shioni goes over my head and hits a witch beside me. The witch begins gasping before she becomes a statue, then crumbles into a pile of stone and dust.

Elizaveta uncaps a set of throwing stars and chucks them at the witch nearest her. The witch grabs Elizaveta by the throat and squeezes. Elizaveta's arms fall to her sides. She becomes immobile, paralyzed by the witch's spell. The witch laughs as she tightens her grip on Elizaveta's throat and yanks upward, attempting to rip her head from her body.

I give a wild yell and shoot. The bullet enters the side of the witch's head. She lets go of Elizaveta and stumbles to the side before crashing onto the ground.

Blood spills everywhere out the wound, leaking onto the white snow and staining it with red. Elizaveta, still paralyzed, falls backward onto the carnage like a rigid board. The blood goes splashing everywhere, and the witch's body dissolves into dust.

A wicked laugh sounds behind me. I turn to see Lidia venture out of the tent. Her cloak catches the blood pool and passes over Elizaveta as she stands before me, smearing red across my friend's face.

"They're disposable. Witches of little power." Lidia waves her hands at her fallen companions. "However, that's not the case with me."

Lidia raises her hands. My companions freeze on the spot. Bryn's trapped in midair, her mouth open, legs spread in a long jump. Shioni's still casting a spell at her two foes, who step backward and observe Lidia nervously. They're afraid of her.

She raises her hand. It smokes dangerously as she ventures toward me. "Oh, don't worry Lysandra. It won't hurt. Much."

She gives another heartless laugh. "I'm just messing with you. It's going to hurt a lot, and I'm going to enjoy every moment of it."

She's footsteps away. Before I can respond I'm knocked aside, and it's not by Lidia. Someone else pushed me out of the way. I look up, whipping my hair out of my face.

I can smell his familiar, beloved scent intermingle with burning flesh and black smoke. Lisar's agonized screams pierce through my very core as Lidia sinks her burning hand into his chest, singing away the skin and muscle so she can rip out his heart.

ELEVEN

*L*isar's screams increase in intensity as Lidia's spell burns through his clothes. I watch as his flesh becomes blackened in the form of a handprint, burning away into Lidia's mark. The only thing that I can hear is Lisar's tortured cries...

I punch her as hard as I can, and she goes sprawling to the ground. To my disappointment she's still moving, though moaning in pain. She *must* be strong. A punch like that could've shattered concrete.

Lisar falls to his knees. His trembling fingers hover over the gaping wound. He's afraid to touch it. Lidia burned through most of his muscles. A few seconds more and she'd have torched his ribcage.

"Lisar..." I don't know what to do. This wound is bad. My eyes water as I look up at him. "Why'd you come after me? You know you can't fight."

Lisar gasps in pain. "I couldn't let you go alone. We're a team."

Snow flies everywhere as three snowmobiles come to a stop. Kipcha, Rosa, and Georgie have arrived. Unable to shift, they fight with guns, shooting at the witches that are still alive. The witches vanish before the wolves can take them down.

Though still stunned, Lidia gives me a delirious grin from her place on the ground. Her eyes are locked on the hole in Lisar's chest.

"It'll always be there, Lysandra. Now when you look at him you'll think of me, and my hand on his heart."

"You bitch." I get up, to hurt Lidia as she's hurt me, but Lisar grabs my wrist. He cries out in pain from the effort. At his touch, I hold back. I hate Lidia, but Lisar needs me.

She snickers. "Bye, Lysandra. I'll see you soon."

Lidia disappears. As she does so, the others unfreeze. Bryn comes down from her leap and crashes on the ground. The spell Shioni was casting flies out of her hands and hits no one. Elizaveta is able to move again. She wrinkles her nose at the blood that has soaked through her hair and clothes.

"Shioni!" I immediately call for her. "Lisar's hurt!"

Seemingly dazed from the freezing spell, Shioni stumbles over to us. As she observes the wound, her face becomes troubled.

Bryn shoots me a dirty look. I can't help but wither inside. This is my fault. Bryn told me this was a trap, but I didn't listen. Now look what's happened.

"This is beyond what my magic can heal," Shioni mutters. "But I might be able to…"

Shioni scoops a pile of snow off the ground and presses it to Lisar's wound. Lisar emits a horrible cry as Shioni twists the snow into the mottled flesh. The snow smokes and melts as it touches Lisar's burn. It drips down his abs slowly as he screams.

"What are you doing to him!?" I yelp. I go to wrench her hand off of him, but Kipcha and Rosa start forward and hold me back.

Shioni lets the snow drop. The white pile, once so pure, is now covered in blood and blackened flesh. I am amazed at the result; Lisar's wound has healed, with nothing more than a faint burn mark in resemblance of a hand right in the middle of it. My wolf sways on the spot, whiter than the tundra.

"He needs rest." Shioni stands up and puts her hands on her hips. "We have to get him back. Along with all of us. We won't be safe until we're inside Salkovia's walls."

"We still won't be safe!" Bryn shouts. "Valentina is out there *right now*, watching us! We already played into another one of her traps, what makes you think we won't fall into another?"

"Bryn. Please." Lisar's voice is weak. At her brother's pleading, Bryn shuts up.

"I'll get a snowmobile," Kipcha says. "Getting the Alpha back is the first priority."

Kipcha drives the snowmobile over to Lisar. He helps his friend stand, though Kipcha has to pick him up to set him on the snowmobile. My wolf flushes. I can tell Lisar is embarrassed at having to be helped. At the moment, Lisar is so weak. What did Lidia do to him?

"I apologize for the false information, sincerely," Elizaveta says quietly to me as Lisar is loaded onto the vehicle. "I've pushed you too hard to be on the offensive. Clearly we need to be more careful about how we confront these witches."

"It was my doing. I was the one who decided we should hold a surprise attack," I mumble.

Once he's onboard, Lisar looks to me. I avoid the eyes of the others and clamber onto the snowmobile.

"You're gonna have to hold onto me, even though it hurts," I say softly.

"I'll manage," he grunts out. He wraps his arms around my waist, though gingerly. "I'm not a pansy."

I look to the others. "Are you guys gonna be fine out here?"

"We'll be fine," Bryn growls. "Just go."

My mouth becomes a thin line. Fine. I want to jet out of there, but I start off at a slow pace and work up to speed so I don't jostle my boyfriend around. I cringe every time we hit a bump. Lisar's yelps of pain accompany it. It's such a short ride, but it feels like forever with the heat of Lisar's wound against my back.

I practically break down the doors to Salkovia when we get there. The eyes of the vampires who open the gate narrow when they see Lisar slumped against me, but they make no comment. One thing I like about Salkovians. They know when to keep their mouth shut.

Unlike *some* people. "By Dracula. What happened to him?"

Tomlien's eyes are wide as he sees me support Lisar as we stumble into the House of Antov. "Where'd you guys go?"

"Ask your girlfriend," I say harshly. Tomlien's face becomes outraged, but I turn Lisar the other way and shuffle down the hall toward our room. I shouldn't be taking my frustration out on Tom, but he's so blasted nosy. Can't he tell this isn't the right time?

After an eternity, I finally lay Lisar down on the bed. His face is still scrunched up in agony, though he doesn't seem to be hurting as much as he was before.

"I've gotta get your clothes off," I whisper, bending over him and working on the zipper. His jacket's destroyed.

"Be my guest. You're more than welcome to." Lisar gives me a rogue smile. Even through the injury, Lisar manages to make the first joke he's told in days. It lifts my spirits a little.

"Perv. I meant your parka and shirt." I can't manage a laugh, just a murky smile. He wiggles uncomfortably on the bed as I start pulling away the clothes. Huge chunks of fabric come off in frayed and burnt pieces. Sitting up is a challenge, but he has to in order to slip off the parka. I tear what's left of the shirt in half so he doesn't have to pull it over his head.

What's left is the familiarity of Lisar's bare chest, left with a large red blemish resembling Lidia's hand.

I want to cry just looking at it.

Lisar catches my expression. "It's not that bad. Really."

"Liar." I sit beside him on the bed. I feel utterly defeated right now.

"It's getting better." He looks at me. "I can tell Shioni's magic is working. The pain gets less and less every second."

"You'll be scarred for life."

"Hey. It's no big deal." He leans against me. "It's just a mark. Who cares? I'm alive. That's the important thing."

"I care." My whole body feels like a deflated balloon, limp and weak. "You were perfect, and I ruined you."

"You're being overdramatic. I'm fine." Lisar sweeps his other hand across my cheek, brushing back loose strands to nestle his fingers lovingly in my hair. "I don't care about this. We're both okay."

"Why did you do that for me?" I wipe my face quickly; I really don't want to cry right now.

"I'm still the Alpha. I need to protect my mate." Lisar grimaces as he shifts. "It doesn't matter that I'm not strong like before. It's still my duty to make sure nothing happens to you. If that means taking things in your place, then I'm cool with that."

"I've been so worried about you. You haven't been eating, or sleeping, and you've barely been talking to me..." I can't help that my words come out rushed.

"I'm sorry I checked out for a few weeks," Lisar whispers. He outlines my ear with his thumb. "It wasn't fair to you."

I squeeze his hand. "It's okay. I understand why you did."

"It's not okay. I was weird for a little while." He makes a face.

"But I understand why. You just lost your mother, your home and your pack a few weeks ago, and now you've lost a big part of who you are," I say.

Lisar takes a deep breath. Slowly, he sits up so that his legs are hanging off the bed. One of his ankles curls around mine and becomes interlocked. "There are things I'm willing to sacrifice in order to be with you," he says. "And it looks like one of those could be being a wolf."

"But you love being a wolf," I protest. "This curse has changed you. It's forced you and the others to become something you're not."

"I'm not gonna lie, it sucks. Like, majorly sucks." He lets out a sigh. "But I'm not different. The curse is something that's *happened* to me, but it hasn't *become* me. If it's something I can't change, I'll learn to deal."

"You mean that?" I ask, astonished.

"Of course I do. I can't change into a wolf, but I still love hunting. I love being in nature, and running with the wind. The wolf is still inside me."

He shrugs. "I just have to find other ways to satisfy him until we find a cure. Going after you and stopping Lidia from hurting you made him come alive again. What she did to me hurt, but I'll take the pain over this hole I feel inside myself. I can still *be* a wolf. I just can't shift into one, if that makes sense."

I sit back. I gnaw on my lip for a moment as thoughts churn inside my head. The decision seems so clear now, and so right. "Then… if you're willing to sacrifice being a wolf for me, I'm willing to make some compromises for you."

"Are you saying what I think you're saying?" Lisar asks. He's become very still… a wolf seconds away from latching onto his prize.

"I am," I say. "The answer is yes. Yes, Lisar, I'll marry you."

"All right!" Lisar launches forward. He puts a hand on the back of my head and draws me inward for a warm, romantic kiss.

As my mouth moves against him, the thought crosses my mind that I love him, in a way that makes the words sound insignificant. I love him more than what I can comprehend, more than what can be told in a story or within the pages of a novel. Despite our star-crossed romance, this was meant to be.

Some things are just beyond us. This unexplainable connection I have with Lisar has gone beyond the magic of wolves and vampires and has transcended into something more. It has changed me forever. I'm a completely new person because of the love I have for him. Everything in myself and in my life has become new, and completely for the better.

I'm not willing to allow anything to take that away from us. Let Valentina and her army come. I doubt even she could break us apart now.

"I knew you couldn't resist me for long." Lisar's completely upright on the bed, totally sunny. It's like he's forgotten all about the wound on his chest. "When should we have the wedding? I don't want to wait."

"My birthday is coming up," I say cheerfully. "It's on December 21, the winter solstice. I would love to have the wedding that day, right before Christmas. It would be the best birthday gift ever, being married to you."

"I'm fine with a winter wedding," Lisar says eagerly. If he had a tail, he'd be wagging it. He's nearly bouncing on the bed.

"You need to calm down." I laugh. Joy has returned to me now. "You're going to hurt yourself more."

"I'm not so hurt that I can't do this." Lisar takes the small, familiar black box out of his pocket. Ever since he asked me the first time he's always carried it with him, waiting. Now the moment has arrived. Carefully, he slips the garnet ring on my right ring finger.

"How did you know Russians wore their wedding rings on their right hand?" I ask, surprised.

"I looked it up. I wanted to make sure I did it right." His eyes sparkle. "Now we just have to figure out how to tell everybody!"

The magical moment dulls a little. What *will* everyone think? Will Serghei disapprove? How about Bryn, or Tomlien? After all, a vampire and a wolf in love is one thing, but marriage? How could they expect it to work out?

It doesn't matter. I'm marrying Lisar whether they like it or not.

There's a knock on our door. "Looks like we don't have much time to celebrate," I say.

Before Lisar can tell whoever it is to come in, the door flies open. Kipcha stands in its stead, gripping the doorknob so hard that it looks like it's going to dent under his fingers. There's a huge grin on his face. Kipcha usually isn't so rude. What's going on?

"Thanks for barging in on us!" Lisar's loud voice is like a bark, happy and light. "We could've been having a moment just now!"

"Uh, I didn't think so, since you couldn't even get on the snowmobile earlier without help." Kipcha's expression doesn't darken, nor does his smile falter. He appears almost as delighted as we are. How can that be so?

"What's going on? It must be important," I say curiously.

"It's good news, finally," Kipcha says quickly. "Shioni wanted me to tell you to come right away. She may have found a cure."

TWELVE

*L*isar immediately gets up from the bed. He gasps in pain, but I lunge out to catch him before he crashes back down.

"Help me with him, won't you?" I ask Kipcha. The beta comes forward and hitches his shoulder under Lisar's arm. Together, we help him hobble toward the doorway.

"Are you sure you're strong enough?" Kipcha asks. "Lysandra and I can go."

"I'm not missing this," he says, teeth clenched. "If there's a cure, I want to know now."

People make way for us when we enter Shioni's room. Everyone's in here; Bryn, Tom, the wolves, Elizaveta... and Serghei. He raises an eyebrow when he notices the garnet ring on my right finger.

Darn. I was hoping he wouldn't notice that, but you can't get anything past the old Russian vampire. At least he has the common sense not to bring it up now, but he gives me a *we need to talk about this* look as we pass him by and settle Lisar on a cot. His black eyes are hard and his body is rigid.

Thankfully, nobody else notices the glistening engagement ring on my hand. They're all waiting on tenterhooks as to what Shioni has to say.

She turns away from a cauldron bubbling with a purple potion, the same one that has been cooking since we got here. I wonder what Shioni's brewing. Georgie nearly knocks it over, but Shioni gasps and flounders for it, catching the cauldron just before it splatters all over the floor. She glares at Georgie, and he shrinks away.

Whatever it is, it must be important.

Something else draws my attention; Bryn and Tomlien are on opposite sides of the room. At first, I think it's just because of the enchantment Bryn's under and they're taking extra precautions, until I notice that there are tearstains under Bryn's eyes. They must've had a fight, a big one.

"Right," Shioni says. "I've been doing a bit of research, and after analyzing the wolf's blood I discovered that Valentina's potion didn't *take away* the ability of the wolves to shift, just blocked it. You guys still have the power to change, but the block must be removed before you can."

"Okay, so how do we do that?" Lisar asks impatiently. "Can you cast a spell or something?"

"There is a way. I can make a potion out of three ingredients. One of which must be wolf's blood uncontaminated by the curse, which we have." She glances at Bryn. "The other two ingredients, however, are very difficult to come by. Nearly impossible, in fact."

"Can we get our paws on them?" Rosa has stepped forward; she's even more adamant then Lisar.

Shioni sighs. "Possibly. The first ingredient is Fane's Ivy. It's a plant that's rumored to contain the magic of the wolf god himself. The other is Love's Breath, a flower from which I must have the petals to bring the spell to life. Yet these two ingredients can only be found within the Russian Taiga, grown by only one witch. Baba Yaga."

"*Baba Yaga?*" Half the room gasps in surprise.

I feel like this is all a joke, though there's nothing funny about it. "Baba Yaga? Isn't she just an old Russian fairy tale?" I ask skeptically.

"No." Shioni shakes her head. "She's real, and the most powerful witch alive. She's stronger than Valentina by tenfold."

Shioni starts to pace. "Baba Yaga is a witch unlike any ever seen before. She must be at least a thousand years old by now. Maybe even more. She has immense experience and wisdom gained in magic after such a long experience."

"How can that be? In all my years I've never heard of such a creature who could exist for thousands of years," Serghei asks.

"Witches are not immortal, but like vampires, have exceptionally long lives," Shioni explains. "If a witch is powerful enough she can use magic to extend her lifespan. Baba Yaga has for centuries."

"Is there a descendent of Baba Yaga, perhaps, that could help us instead?" Tomlien asks hopefully. Bryn recoils at the sound of his voice.

"Witches don't have children, nor parents. They're created by magic," Shioni says simply, like this explains everything.

"Okay, hold on." Lisar puts up his hands. "You're going to have to explain how witches work to the rest of us lower magical creatures. If you would, please."

Shioni gives a great sigh, as if this is all common knowledge and annoying for her to recount. "When a witch dies, a baby appears in the Pool of Mystic Dwellings, an enchanted water basin Baba Yaga lives by. The baby is always female, always magical. Baba Yaga takes the baby and tends to it until the coven the dead witch was a part of writes to Baba Yaga requesting a replacement. The coven will raise the child until she is old enough to be placed in a wolf pack or vampire coven, usually whoever is willing to pay the most."

Shioni drops her gaze. "There was an exception, in my case. The pack witch died early as a result of the war between the shifters and vampires. I was five when I was sent to live with them. Another witch accompanied me, and stayed there to teach me magic until I was strong enough to handle things on my own."

Shioni crosses the room. "There are four main covens. Well, three now, since Valentina destroyed my own." Shioni's face hollows. "The replacement children all went to her own coven."

"How can that be?" Bryn asks. Concern shadows her face for her handmaiden. "Wouldn't the coven just die out?"

"There must always be the same number of witches in the world," Shioni says. "Even if you managed to eliminate all of them, more babies would appear in the Pool. No one dares to fight a war against witches. It is a fight you cannot win."

Lisar and I stare at each other. A war of witches. An impossible thing to think about, and yet, it is right here at our door.

"Baba Yaga isn't evil. But neither is she good," Shioni says. "She's a neutral force that works according to her own will. She doesn't care about the affairs of vampires or wolves. She hardly bothers with the matters of her own kind."

Shioni gnaws at her fingernails anxiously. "She might help us. But she could destroy us just as easily."

The witch bites her nails to the quick, drawing blood. Though it's only a tiny pinprick, I can smell it all the way across the room. Already, I know the idea of searching for Baba Yaga makes Shioni nervous. Very nervous.

"Do we have a choice?" Lisar asks. "This is our only chance. Do you know where to find her? The taiga is thousands of kilometers wide. That's a big area to look."

Shioni nods slowly. "I have a guess. It's a long shot, though."

"I don't think we should leave until the Alpha is stable enough to travel," Kipcha says, eyeing Lisar carefully.

"I don't need to be babied, Kip. By Fane, what are you, my mother?" Lisar growls.

"No, I agree with Kipcha." Shioni grabs a roll of parchment from one of her many bookcases. She unfurls it, and lays it on a table near her bedside. It's a map. "We'll have to search a very large area. We're going to need everyone."

Shioni picks up a wooden spoon. She stirs the purple cauldron three times in one direction before stirring three times in another. "Everyone needs to get some rest. We'll leave in a couple of days."

The group begins to fan out. Serghei doesn't stick around, which surprises me. He merely gives a stern stare over his shoulder at me before leaving the room. Kipcha lifts Lisar again, and the two friends start shuffling down the hallway.

I don't miss the fact that Bryn and Tom head in separate directions as they leave.

"Hey Lisar, I'll be along in a bit," I say, watching Bryn. She rounds a corner in a flurry, obviously upset.

"You noticed too, huh?" he asks. He eyes his sister as she walks away. "Okay. Let me know what's going on."

"I will." I kiss him on the cheek before pattering after Bryn. I make sure to keep my distance while following the she-wolf. To my surprise she leads me to the same place I found Lisar, to the fountain in the greenhouse.

Bryn sits on the edge of the fountain and starts crying. She puts her head in her hands as tears roll from her eyes. Her shoulders start to shake. My soul weeps for Bryn; she's really hurting.

"Bryn?" I say cautiously. I creep around the edge of the fountain, fiddling with my hands. "What's wrong?"

"Go away!" she shouts. She looks up from her hands and gives me a glare. "I don't want you here!"

"If that was true you would've already told me to leave you alone. You knew I followed you. You could smell my scent," I say.

I sit down next to her. She doesn't stop crying, but the tears slow. "Tell me what happened."

"Tommy and I broke up," she says harshly. "Happy you know? Now go tell everyone else, so I don't have to."

"Oh no." I frown. "I'm sorry, Bryn. I didn't think he'd do that. He seemed crazy about you."

"He didn't break up with me. I broke up with him." Bryn sniffs.

"What?" I reel backwards in surprise. "Why'd you do that?"

"Because we can't be together!" she shouts. Her screams echo against the glass walls. "It doesn't matter that I've bonded with him, it doesn't matter that I love him, nothing matters when it comes down to this curse! All it does is make me despise him!"

"So you have bonded with him, then." I keep my hands folded calmly in my lap.

"You already knew I did. Lisar did too." She smears her nose on the back of her sleeve. "I just didn't want to admit it."

"That's not a bad thing. If you bonded with him it literally means you're meant to be together," I say, trying to comfort her. "I'm sure we can work this out. We just have to kill Valentina and then—"

"You don't understand how painful this is for me!" Bryn blurts out. "If I'm not with him the bond hurts, but if I am with him the curse hurts, too! Even without the magic, do you understand what it's like to not be able to touch the person you love? To not be able to kiss him, to hug him, to even hold his hand?"

Bryn's teary eyes burn with jealousy. "No. Of course you don't. You and Lisar are always all over each other. Well, let me tell you that this curse is complete torture. I hate it. I can't stand it any longer. That's why I broke up with Tommy. I just don't want to do it anymore."

"That's not going to make the bond go away, Bryn," I say firmly. "Don't give up on love, on Tommy. He's not willing to give up on you."

"*Get out!*" Bryn gets up from the fountain. She grabs a flowery pot and throws it at me. I launch upwards and out of my seat. The pot misses, and shatters on the edge of the granite.

Bryn picks up another one and chucks it my way. "I hate you! I hate Tommy, too! I wish I never got involved with stupid vampires!"

I skirt out of there before Bryn smashes a vase against my head. That would just cause another row between her and her brother, and the last thing we need is another argument going around the house.

Bryn's loud sobs turn into howls as I close the greenhouse door behind me. I can hear them all the way down the hall.

Bryn didn't mean what she said. She doesn't hate me, and she definitely doesn't hate Tomlien. She's just suffering from a broken heart.

An engagement and a break up all in one day. It seems wrong that Lisar and I are so happy when Bryn and Tomlien are miserable.

I clench my fists so tightly that my nails bite into the skin. This isn't fair. There has to be a way to end Valentina so we can lift this curse. I won't rest until that witch has been taken down. No matter what the cost, I'm going to make Valentina pay for doing this to my friend.

I just don't know how.

THIRTEEN

hree days later, Lisar is finally healthy enough to travel. The wound has slowed him down, and without his shifter abilities it doesn't heal quickly, but he's become restless. Without the power to change into a wolf, he's become like a caged animal in a zoo. Hopefully that ends today.

We gather together at the doors to the House of Antov just as twilight falls. Serghei, Tomlein, Elizaveta, Shioni, and all the wolves are there, reporting for duty.

There are two large, male vampires with Elizaveta I don't know. Both are around my age or a little older, though they're particularly gigantic and armed with enough weapons to supply a platoon.

"This is Fyor and Valeri," Elizaveta says, gesturing to them. "They will be our protection."

Fyor gives us a friendly smile, clutching his AK-47, but Valeri definitely doesn't want to be here. He holds his head high above the wolves, like he considers himself above them.

We embark the snow mobiles for the airport, then board the plane once we arrive. Thankfully, we don't encounter any witches along the way. By the time the plane lands near the taiga, I'm starting to wonder why it's going so well.

Once there, we board a large utility vehicle. Two benches line the bed, which is covered by a circular sheet of canvas stretched over several bars that loop over our heads. I sit with Lisar near the back, while the rest of them pile in behind us. It's a tight fit.

One of the vampires from Elizaveta's satellites is driving. She bangs her hand on the back of the Jeep's window, and off we go.

"Get away from me," Rosa snarls. She scooches a few inches in the opposite direction as Valeri takes a (reluctant) spot next to her, the only one that's left. "I'm not sitting next to a vampire."

"The pleasure is all mine," Valeri growls back. "I don't want to sit next to you, either. You smell like a dog."

"Two peas in a pod, aren't they?" I whisper to Lisar.

"They're not the only ones," he grumbles back. "Those two are annoying."

His attention is fixed on Georgie and Fyor, who are talking their heads off about everything and anything. I haven't heard them shut up since we got on the plane. Apparently, they like each other. Well-mannered and optimistic people can be found within all races, I suppose.

Personally, I'm glad for the noise they make. The misery Tom and Bryn have dragged along with them makes it awkward for everyone. The lonesome, lost looks they give each other make it seem like one or both of them is going to break down and cry or start screaming at any moment. I wish they'd chosen to stay behind. Tomlien takes the very back of the Jeep, while Bryn decides to wedge herself between Lisar and the wall at the front. It crushes Lisar and I against each other.

"Bryn, why don't you sit near Tomlien?" Lisar suggests. I bristle, knowing what he's trying to do. "There's not a lot of room up here, and there's a spot between Rosa and Valeri so you don't have to touch him."

"If I have to sit by him I'd rather run," Bryn responds sharply.

"It's not that bad, Bryn. Maybe you guys can work it out," Lisar offers.

"Don't tell me what to do."

Lisar rolls his eyes and leans against the bar of the Jeep. He's tried convincing Bryn to go back to Tomlien several times, but she won't listen. Once Bryn's made up her mind about something, there's no telling her otherwise.

Serghei is sitting across from us. His gaze is fixed on me. It has been the entire trip. He's staring me down like we're about to go to war or something.

I've been avoiding Serghei since his eyes caught the ring. I don't know whether to expect a lecture or congratulations. The uncertainty of it has made me reluctant to talk to him.

The wind coming through the canvas of the Jeep is messing with my hair. I start braiding it. As I do so, the garnet ring flickers in the darkness, catching Georgie's attention.

"What's that?" Georgie asks curiously. He peers forward, narrowing his eyes at the ring.

"By Dracula," Elizaveta breathes when she notices. "That's an engagement ring, isn't it?"

The vehicle goes silent. All attention is on me. It's like everyone in the Jeep is holding their breath. I glance at Lisar; he nods his head encouragingly. I feel my mouth go dry. "Yes. Lisar and I are getting married."

The response provides gasps. Noise erupts within the trailer, along with questions and loud shouts of excitement.

"You guys are engaged?" Georgie's expression is bright and happy. "Congratulations!"

"Congrats, man," Kipcha says, reaching out to clap Lisar on the shoulder. He glances at me, gives a roguish grin and adds, "Took you long enough to give him the answer he wanted, didn't it?"

My mouth drops open. Kipcha knew all along Lisar was going to ask, didn't he?

Of course he did. Lisar would never keep secrets from his beta. I'm betting Kipcha helped him with it!

"You two plan to be married? This is good news," Elizaveta says. "But you haven't known each other very long, have you?"

"Hey, when you know you know," Lisar says, shrugging. He nudges me playfully with his shoulder. "I always knew, ever since I first met her. Now's as good a time as ever, don't you think?"

"This is incredible," Shioni whispers. "A wolf and a vampire, getting married? I'd never thought I'd see the day!"

"We know." I reach down and grab Lisar's hand. "We get that this has never been done before. But we're willing to make that commitment and take the leap." I swallow. "It's the one thing that'll show Dragomir that we're united against him permanently."

"When is it? Do you plan on having the wedding soon?" Elizaveta asks curiously.

"We, uh..." I look at Lisar. "We were planning on having it December 21. My birthday."

"That's so soon!" Shioni says in surprise. "Only a little more than a month!"

"If it is to be so, we need to get things ready," Elizaveta says, taking the lead. "We must prepare the church, and organize a banquet. We shall have a wedding for our csarina like none Salkovia has ever seen!"

"Hold on," I laugh. "We're getting ahead of ourselves. We need to find the cure for this curse first."

Elizaveta completely ignores me. She launches into discussions of cake and decorations with Shioni, while Fyor and Georgie discuss all the food they hope will be served and the party afterwards. Even Rosa seems a little interested in chatting about our engagement, though she's still pointedly ignoring Valeri.

Lisar leans in to whisper against my ear. "I think we just gave up our own wedding planning to these people," he says. His eyes are smiling.

"I'm surprised they're taking it so well," I murmur back. "I thought they'd have a fit."

But not everyone is happy at the news. Bryn's face started burning the second she noticed the ring. Now her arms and legs are crossed. She refuses to look at Lisar or me, staring at the wall like she could melt a hole in it with her glare.

Tomlien's gripping his rifle so hard that his knuckles are turning white. His mouth is a tight line, body paralyzed in the moment. If someone touched him, he'd go off like a bomb.

I can only imagine how he feels. First I put him off and did everything I could to stop the wedding between him and I, and now I'm jumping into a marriage with Lisar. Add that to the terrible fact he's lost Bryn to something that's completely out of his control.

Serghei doesn't say anything, nor does his expression change. His non-response gives me no hints on whether or not he approves. It's maddening.

Finally, the arrival at our destination puts a halt on the wedding planning. We find ourselves surrounded by conifer trees, with snow and plants as far as the eye can see. Besides the forest, it's completely barren out here... I'm sure no one populates this area for hundreds of kilometers. How are we supposed to find Baba Yaga?

Valeri hands out two-way radios, along with extra batteries so we can communicate. Everyone is clutching onto their weapons tightly. I don't blame them. The forest itself seems intimidating.

Shioni's good cheer is gone. She's on high-alert as she leads the way through the woods. "Everyone, pick a partner and distance yourselves out," she instructs. "We'll make up more ground if we split up."

Before I can pair off with Lisar, Serghei grabs me by the arm. Lisar watches Serghei pull me away as he's forced to team up with Bryn. Serghei drags me to the outskirts of the group until we're nearly alone in the taiga, only able to hear the others in the distance.

"Grandfather, what are you doing?" I'm only able to wrench my arm away from him once he lets go. For an old vampire, he has a strong grip.

"Your engagement, Lysandra." Serghei faces me, the lines on his face deepenin and dark eyes growing wary. "When did this happen?"

Here we go. I take a deep breath. "Lisar proposed to me weeks ago, the same night we escaped the den," I say. "I originally told him no, but after he got hurt when he took Lidia's spell for me, I realized that life is short and that we might not have forever like I thought. I changed my mind and told him yes."

"I see." I expected him to be stern, or disapproving, but he's not.

His only expression is worried. In turn, it makes me anxious. "I can certainly understand your reasoning."

"Please say you approve, Grandfather." I clutch his arm in a pleading way. "He makes me so happy, and he's a good person. You know he'll take care of me."

"I understand how you feel, and there is nothing wrong with the boy." He sighs. "But I'm concerned you're rushing into things. You're so young. You've barely tasted what life has to offer."

"You and Grandmother were married at eighteen." I put my hands on my hips. "What makes this any different?"

"Times were different then, and we were both vampires. This has never been done before." Serghei reaches out, and clenches my hand. "I can only stand behind you if I'm certain that this is what you want."

I nod. "Yes. It is. Right time or not, it's going to happen eventually, and I want it to now. Grandfather, I'm in love with him."

Serghei and I always had that special kind of relationship where we could be honest. Right now, there's nothing truer or more vulnerable about me. Everyone can see that it's obvious I love Lisar. Admitting it to people out loud, though, has never been something I've felt strong enough to do unless I was in a life-or-death situation and I had no choice but to reveal my feelings.

This is different. This is pouring my heart out to my family and hoping, *praying* they'll listen.

Serghei's eyes are kind. "I understand, Granddaughter. But I insist you even consider waiting. A few years, or months even. You have only known this wolf for so short a time, and time has a way of changing people. There will be plenty of opportunities to get married later, after the war."

I shake my head sadly. "There isn't going to *be* an after the war, Grandfather. Dragomir will rule always."

"It may seem that way," Serghei says softly. "But I still believe you have a chance of defeating him. He isn't content to let you roam free forever."

I look away. "We'll see."

Serghei rubs his beard tiredly. "This is your decision. If this is what you feel you must do, I will stand behind you all the way."

A smile brightens on my face. I rush forward and embrace Serghei in a tight hug. "Thank you, Grandfather. You don't know how much this means to me."

He merely grunts in reply, and strokes my hair. I understand this is hard for him, letting me go. After all, look what happened to my mother after she married Dragomir.

But this is different. Lisar is nothing like my father, and he never will be. I'll be safe and happy with Lisar. I hope, in time, Serghei will realize that, and trust this wolf with my heart.

We start walking again, this time actually focusing on searching for Baba Yaga. A few minutes in, Serghei asks, "When you accepted his proposal, did you give any thought to how you would have children?"

"Children?" It piques my interest. "I don't know. I suppose I didn't. I doubt a vampire and a werewolf would be able to conceive a child together."

"Hm." Serghei seems sorrowful. "Is this something you're willing to sacrifice?"

"I suppose so." The thought of not being able to have children with Lisar makes me sad… very sad. But I wouldn't want to bring any kids into a world where Dragomir rules, anyway. "But it's worth it, to be with him."

I'm glad Serghei says nothing more on the subject. We search for a few hours, and stay quiet. I try to put the thought of babies out of my mind. Starting a family isn't something that's important right now. We have more pressing priorities at hand.

Eventually the radios start screaming, telling us to come back. Purple sparks shoot up in the air about a kilometer off. Shioni, signaling us. We meet up with the others in a clearing where Shioni sent off the sparks. Everyone is accounted for, but we haven't found anything.

"This is no good," Kipcha says. He shakes his head. "We could spend weeks searching the forest and never find her."

"We'll find her," Shioni promises. "Baba Yaga knows we're here. It's only a matter of time before she decides to come out."

Nobody says anything. Waiting for an immortal witch who has all the time in the world to reveal herself doesn't sound very hopeful.

"Let's walk in a group," Shioni suggest. "Maybe we'll draw her attention that way."

Since none of us have any better ideas, we let Shioni lead the way. The conversation is kept quiet. This is starting to feel like a wild goose chase.

"Serghei talked to me about the wedding," I whisper to Lisar. We've sectioned ourselves off in the back of the group, away from everyone.

"I got a rant from Bryn, too," Lisar responds. "It doesn't matter. We've made the decision. I'm sticking to it."

I nod in agreement. Ahead of us, people are swapping stories about Baba Yaga.

"I heard she flies around in a mortar and pestle," Rosa says, like she knows it all.

"No, she *wields* a pestle and flies around in a mortar," Valeri says condescendingly. "Trust a wolf to get it wrong."

"What do you know about it?" Rosa snarls.

"More than you! I'm a Russian. You don't know anything about our culture. You're just a *Romanian*." Valteri snorts the word.

"When I was growing up my mother used to tell me Baba Yaga lived in a hut on chicken legs, one that ran around the forest like it was alive," Fyor adds eagerly. "Legend goes she might help or hinder anyone who comes into her presence. She could give you a pile of gold or turn you into a toad. You just don't know, with Baba Yaga."

"Cut it out you guys," Georgie says nervously. "You're starting to scare me."

"Boo!" Kipcha shouts right behind Georgie. He shoots straight into the air and flounders like a fish, landing into Fyor's arms.

Georgie blushes. Fyor puts him down and Lisar shoves the group apart. "Quit playing around, you guys. We're never going to find—"

"Lysandra, Lysandra."

Lisar's words are cut off by a mysterious voice that echoes my name. The sound vibrates off the trees, bouncing off the trunks until it surrounds me like a trap. The voice is raspy, choked, and quiet.

It is the voice of an old woman.

"Who's there?" I ask. I turn on the spot, but all I see are the dark woods. "How do you know my name? Show yourself!"

The faces of my companions have gone pale with fright. The wolves cower against each other, while the vampires clutch their weapons in fear. Shioni appears she wants to faint.

"Don't play games, child. You know who I am, Lysandra, vampire princess," Baba Yaga whispers. *"You alone must come with me."*

FOURTEEN

he trees part. They literally get up and move, uplifting themselves from the ground and walking on their roots as if they have legs. They separate to make a thin, narrow pathway, one that seems threatening and ominous.

I know Baba Yaga waits at the end of it.

"Venture into my woodlands to find what you seek," Baba Yaga croons. *"But come alone."*

"No." Lisar plants himself in front of me. He grabs me and wraps me tightly in his arms. "No way I'm letting you go by yourself."

"Let go of me, Lisar. I'm stronger than you now," I say, slinking out of his arms. It proves to be a challenge, because he doesn't want to move.

"I have to agree with the Alpha. We don't know what Baba Yaga is planning," Shioni says cautiously. "We may never see you again."

"That's a risk I'm willing to take." I finally manage to escape Lisar's arms, and hold him at a distance.

"Your life isn't worth my powers. I'll stay like this forever to keep you safe!" Lisar hisses. His voice, nearly a growl, almost makes me believe he can change again.

"You might be okay with it, but I'm not sentencing your friends to the same fate," I say harshly. "We're doing this for the pack!"

I look at the wolves. They don't want me to go in there, obviously, but neither do they make any attempt to stop me.

"Lysandra. This is irrational," Serghei argues. He appears firm. "These *are* witches we're talking about."

Serghei's gaze flickers to Shioni, but there's no offense taken. She understands what he means. Serghei reaches forward to restrain me, but before he can I jump onto the path. The tree branches close in around me, forming a gate the others cannot cross.

"Lysandra!" Serghei's eyes are hurt.

"I'm not staying, Grandfather." I start to slowly back away. "Nobody follow me. Wait for me here. If I'm not back by dawn..."

I trail off, because I don't know what to tell them to do if I don't return. I hate the desperate look in Lisar's face, so I turn away and start walking down the path.

As I do so the trees move again, swallowing me up. I can no longer see the others. I'm truly by myself.

I'm glad I can see in the dark, because the pathway's pitch-black. I take slow, steady steps, putting away my pistol. It's no use against a witch, and I'm sure if Baba Yaga wanted me dead, she would've killed me by now.

The pathway seems to get longer and longer, stretching ahead of me with each step. It feels like I've walked forever. "Where are you, Baba Yaga?" I ask.

"*Lysandra*," the voice whispers again. I follow it, and the path twists in another direction. It widens, and the walkway comes to an end in a starlit clearing, one devoid of snow. Flowers grow in circular patches, and green grass shoots up beneath my feet. Winter doesn't come here. It's like a permanent spring.

A hunchbacked figure wearing a tattered, dingy cloak hobbles over a shimmering pool. The moon reflects a circular spot within the water. Without any explanation, it begins to bubble. From the water rises a large flower, purple in color with swirling petals, larger than my torso. It opens slowly to reveal a tiny, naked infant, asleep within the petals. Withered, wrinkled hands reach out and snatch the baby, wrapping it within a swaddle of white fabric and bracing it to her chest.

The figure turns around. I'm faced with an old woman, very old. The lines on her face create a map that tells a story that lasts for ages. Her eyes are gray and drooping, ears large and round. Her long gray hair is tied in two braids that fall over her big belly. A large, round nose is topped with a prominent wart. She smacks her lips; she has no teeth. She looks all the part of a fairy-tale witch that devours children for supper.

I attempt to appear polite. "You must be Baba Yaga."

The old woman nods. The infant doesn't stir in her arms. "That I am."

I gesture to the water. "Is that the Pool of Mystic Dwellings?"

Baba Yaga's eyes flash, and she doesn't reply. I hastily remember not to get involved in the affairs of witches.

I clench my hands together to keep from playing with them. "You called me here. What is it you need?"

"I need nothing from you, vampire princess, but I know you have need of me." Baba Yaga shifts the baby to one arm and waves her other hand my way. "Come. Follow."

I meekly obey. We wind around the garden endlessly, like we're in a maze, until I see the outline of a crooked hut on the horizon. The hut is slumped to one side, and has a roof that's falling apart. Cracks run up the sides of the walls and the windows are broken. There's no way it could stand without magic, but I see that it doesn't stand… it moves. The house literally twists back and forth, like its dancing of its own accord. This is the strangest thing about it, however. Her hut isn't on chicken legs, not as far as I can see.

Baba Yaga opens the door. I step inside and see that the house is packed full to the brim with spell books, vials, and plants in pots. Jars of strange ingredients, such as eyeballs, lizards, spiders, and powders, line the bookshelves. Several cauldrons bubble with multiple potions at once, far more than I believe even Shioni could handle at a time. Everything's in a pell-mell fashion, nothing organized. I have to step over several items to keep from tripping over them, as many of Baba Yaga's things are scattered all over the floor.

Baba Yaga leads me to a different room. Inside are multiple cradles, dozens of them. They line the walls in a uniform fashion, the only thing not in disarray within the house. The cottage isn't that big. I wonder how she's packed all these babies in here, until I realize that Baba Yaga must be making the inside larger with magic.

I gasp when I see multiple Baba Yagas taking care of the children. The Baba Yagas hold the babies, feed them bottles, change them and sing them to sleep. The original Baba Yaga lays the new baby down in an empty cradle, and turns to me.

I shiver. There's not a witch alive that can replicate herself. Not that I know of, at least.

"That's a lot of babies," I remark before mentally smacking myself in the head. By Dracula, why can't I keep quiet? I'm so nervous.

"The Pool has sent me many children as of late," Baba Yaga replies. "Many witches are about to die."

Baba Yaga catches me staring at her clones. "You must get used to enjoying time with yourself, you know," Baba Yaga replies. "Most of the time, you are all you've got."

She shuffles out of the nursery. I follow her back to the main room, glad when she closes the door behind her. All of this seems so unnatural, and I'm a vampire.

The old witch hobbles to a table. She takes out a tiny paring knife and starts chopping up little roots, shrubs, and mushrooms on a cutting board, then slides them into a cauldron that sparks. Each time she adds a new ingredient a voice comes out of it, like the potion is singing. It's very odd.

Minutes pass. I feel awkward, but it's like Baba Yaga has forgotten all about me. She's acting as if I'm not here. I don't want to be rude, but we are on a time limit. I chance speaking. "Pardon me, but I've come to ask—"

"You're looking for Fane's Ivy and Love's Breath. Yes, I have them," Baba Yaga says before I can finish. "I've been growing them for years."

Baba Yaga's cold gaze lifts to me. "Though I'm not sure you deserve them."

My stomach drops. "Deserve them?"

"Yes. Clean out your ears, girl." Baba Yaga shakes her head and adds another ingredient to the pot. A soprano voice lifts out. "The youth of today."

I take a deep breath. "I'm sorry. I really regret taking up your time, or bothering you in the first place, but I need those plants. Just give them to me, and I'll be on my way."

"As I said, I'm not sure yet if you deserve them," Baba Yaga snaps. She puts a lid on the cauldron, and the voices die out.

"What do you mean by that?" I demand. I'm starting to get irritated, which is a bad idea in this situation. There's no way I can take Baba Yaga.

"I don't need to hear rumors to know what Csar Dragomir has done," Baba Yaga says. She turns to a different cauldron, this time plucking feathers from what seems like an invisible bird. The feathers appear in the air as she plucks, and trail into the cauldron where they simmer against a golden liquid. "It would be a grave mistake for me to aid someone who could possibly turn out just like him."

Her words feel like a punch in the gut. "What about you?" *Stop it, Lysandra.* "You're a very powerful witch, the strongest alive! You could defeat Dragomir, but you choose not to!"

"This isn't my war. I learned long ago to stop involving myself in things that weren't my business," she seethes. "Why do you suppose most regard me as a silly children's story? It is best kept that way.

"So you would let an entire race die out, while another is enslaved to a mad dictator?" I ask, shocked.

"If fate wills it? Yes." Baba Yaga shrugs.

"But... but that's so wrong," I say weakly. "How can you stand by and do nothing?"

"Who do you think was the witch who made the deal with Vlad the Impaler to defeat the Ottomans?" Baba Yaga hisses, and I lurch back in surprise. Spittle flies from her cracked lips. "Who do you think gave him and his descendants power over humanity as they drank the blood of others? I believed I was saving lives, only to create a species that exists merely to go to war with another!"

She makes a skeptical noise. The anger fades from her; she goes back to what she was doing. "No. Never again."

I take a slow step toward her. "I don't blame you for creating vampires. I don't blame you for making me, me."

I hesitate, holding my breath. "But if Lisar isn't able to change into a wolf ever again, I *will* blame you. I won't be able to hurt you, or take revenge. But I will hate you forever for it."

"Lisar." Baba Yaga snickers. She picks up a wooden spoon, stirring the golden liquid. "Oh, yes. *The one who shall end the shifter line comes. Borne on winter's first breath. Fair of hair. Blue of eye. Descended from the Romanov Dynasty.*"

Baba Yaga cackles as she stirs the cauldron. Her eyes are alight with a wicked fire.

"The prophecy." The words usher out from my lips in a whisper. "You know it."

"Of course I know it," Baba Yaga says irritably. "If nothing else, watching your chaotic little story unfold is at least entertaining."

"What does it mean?" I fall to my knees in front of her, daring to clutch at her robe. She sneers, but does nothing to stop me. "Tell me."

Baba Yaga looks down to me. "It means that you will either live up to it, or you will not. The prophecy is entirely in your hands. The only doubt in my mind is if you are worthy enough to create the right outcome."

There are tears welling up in my eyes. Right now, I feel like such a failure.

"Please. *Please.*" I take a deep breath, to try and swallow the lump forming in my throat. "My wolf is sick. His pack is sick. He's lost, because he's unable to change. He doesn't know what to do. I will do anything to cure my Alpha. Anything."

Baba Yaga stares. She sets the spoon down. Then she moves beside the cauldron and sweeps her hand over it. "Stand, child."

I get to my feet. Baba Yaga peers into her bubbling brew. "Look into the cauldron," she replies. "How you respond to what's within will determine whether I give you the ingredients or not."

A test? Very well. If I have to prove myself to obtain these ingredients, then so be it. I go to look downward but Baba Yaga smacks a hand on my chest, holding me back.

"Beware," she starts. "The potion will only reveal the truth. I will not be able to take away what you see after it releases you from its spell. If you are not brave enough, turn away now."

"As I said, I will do anything," I reply.

I look downward. At first, it merely appears as before, a golden liquid that swirls and spins.

Then the potion picks up speed. It swirls faster and faster, until it changes into scenes of places I've been and pictures of people I know.

Lisar's face appears. It doesn't take but a second for the golden pool to turn to thick, red blood, blurring out the image of my wolf. I can smell the blood. I can feel it running over me, sucking me in and dripping down my hands.

The taste is utterly familiar. I'm drowning in Lisar's blood.

I scream. The sound is a bloodcurdling cry of horror. I attempt to wrench my eyes away from the golden spell, but too late. I'm unable to escape, trapped within the enchantment as I tumble into a vision of dreams and nightmares.

FIFTEEN

I'm no longer standing in Baba Yaga's hut. I'm floating in a place that is neither the present or the future, suspended above a canvas of white that, slowly, begins to form images below me.

The canvas keeps changing. The first image is one of Salkovia. It's on fire. Buildings collapse and explode by use of spells. Vampires fall under powerful blasts of magic as an army of witches' march on the fortress. Huge holes are blown in the outer wall, and flaming rocks fall from the sky. The snow becomes stained with blood as the witches loom closer and closer to their final destination, the House of Antov.

The canvas changes. It turns from a torn battlefield to a dark forest, a woman with light blonde hair and blue eyes running as fast as she can from an unseen terror, clutching a small bundle in her arms.

"Mother," I whisper, choked. Before my fingertips can reach out to stroke her cheek, the story fades. It's replaced by the sight of the Winter Palace in St. Petersburg. The sky darkens behind it as thunder dances with lightning.

Wolves are everywhere. They scamper from the palace as vampires follow them, but they are not at war. They are running from an unforeseeable demon that lurks within the realm of the palace.

Finally, the canvas rips in half. My head swings from one side to another as I look at the two pieces. They form a jagged picture... me. I'm on the floor of some unknown location, one that looks like a cell, wearing a thin slip that's barely more than a pillowcase. It droops across my bony shoulders.

Sunlight beams through the open bars. The minute the sun touches me, it begins to burn away my skin. It curls backward, creating blooming sores that spread across my body.

There's nowhere for me to hide, no shade to be found within the cell. I scream as the sunlight eats away my flesh, devouring everything. My body turns ashen and black, singeing away to bone and mutilated muscle.

Eventually, the screaming stops. I curl up into a ball on the floor before stilling completely.

I don't have to be told to already know. Death by sunlight. The worst possible way a vampire can be killed.

I'm ripped away from the vision. Pain explodes in my knees as I collapse onto the floor. I'm back in Baba Yaga's hut. Sweat covers me, soaking through my clothes. I'm shaking all over.

Baba Yaga hands me a cup of blood. It's chicken blood, which I hate, but I'm not being picky. I slug down the cup and find myself steadying, though it doesn't help with the anxiety. I feel like I'm going to throw up. What I saw shook me to my very core.

"Is it true?" I ask. My voice has become raspy. I finish the blood and stare at Baba Yaga.

"You've seen the future," Baba Yaga says ominously. "As I said, the spell doesn't lie. What you witnessed will come to pass, should you choose to marry the werewolf."

I swallow. "It doesn't matter," I say. "What will be will be."

Baba Yaga nods solemnly. She reaches out a hand to help me stand. I take it, and find I'm wobbling on my feet. The room is spinning around me. I'm so dizzy.

Baba Yaga strides to a row of potted plants on the windowsill. She plucks two of them from their pots; one, an ivy plant riddled with a mottled design, another a pink flower with petals in the shape of hearts.

"You have passed," Baba Yaga says, pressing the plants into my hands. She folds my fingers over the ingredients. "Don't lose them, for these are all I have and it takes time to bloom them, time that you and your friends do not have."

I manage to perform a wobbly curtsy. "Thank you, Baba Yaga." As I rise, my body finally strengthens. "I appreciate the gift."

"Do not thank me. You paid a heavy price for them." Baba Yaga waves me off. "Follow the winding path round the gardens back to where you came. You shall find your friends waiting for you."

I turn to go. I want to leave this dreadful place as soon as I can. But before I can, Baba Yaga catches my arm. Though she's an old woman, her grip is anything but frail. It's strong... more powerful than even the Alpha's.

"It will be interesting to see your story play out, princess of vampires," Baba Yaga says lowly. "So far you've proven not to disappoint me."

I'm not sure what she means. But I don't have the patience to bother her with more questions that I, most likely, cannot handle the answers to. I lower my eyes and Baba Yaga lets me go. Quietly, as to not wake the babies, I shut the door behind me.

As I wind through the gardens I find my mind brimming with questions, each one more terrifying than the last. The sight of Salkovia under attack by witches was horrifying, but not surprising. It was predictable that would come to pass, the only question being when.

One thing Baba Yaga said above all bothers me. She said those were visions of the future, but my mother's dead. I watched wolves kill her. I attended her funeral. How could she be running from enemies in the future if she's not alive?

Yet the vision of my mother didn't disturb me the most. The sunlight, the sight of my skin melting off my bones and sticking to the floor, was the worst part. Baba Yaga told me that these things were certain. A powerful witch like her doesn't have reason to lie. If I stay with Lisar, my life will come to a very painful end.

I don't know what's more unnerving; that I'm going to die, sometime soon, or that knowing I will doesn't change my decision to marry my wolf prince.

When I reach the Pool of Mystic Dwellings, the trees part again. The pool bubbles just as I enter the thin path of branches and brambles. Another witch will be born soon.

The walk seems much quicker, most likely because I'm distracted by thoughts of what I just saw. Finally, the trees get up and walk out of my way to show the group gathered in the same clearing I left them in, sitting around a small fire. They look up when they hear the sound of trees being uprooted from the earth.

"*Lysandra!*" several people shout at once. The group rushes toward me, surrounding me. Everyone appears relieved. Serghei's shoulders relax; the joy comes back into Lisar's face.

"Did you get the ingredients?" Shioni asks. She shoves her way to the front of the group and clutches her dress.

"Yes, I got them," I say. I open my hands to reveal the plants. The group starts cheering when they see them. I give them to Shioni, who tucks them inside a pocket in her robe.

Lisar notices the tone in my voice. He raises an eyebrow, but I don't respond.

"Well done, Lysandra!" Rosa congratulates, and I'm momentarily taken aback by her kindness. "I didn't think you could do it!"

"What was it like in Baba Yaga's house?" Georgie asks eagerly. "Was it on chicken legs? Is she as scary as we thought?"

The others begin prompting me with questions, but I don't answer. I can barely understand the words they're saying.

"Hey guys, leave her alone," Lisar says, shoving the others away. "She'll talk about it later."

The group moans collectively. Serghei's figured out there's something wrong, too. He takes charge and commands attention.

"We should head back," he says. "The light will dawn soon, and we vampires should be on the plane before that happens."

Everyone reluctantly agrees. We begin venturing through the taiga again. The wolves come near, to keep harassing me with questions, but Lisar gives them a glare only an Alpha can achieve. They end up roaming away.

"What's wrong?" Lisar whispers, out of earshot of the others. "What did Baba Yaga do to you?"

"Nothing," I lie. "I'm fine."

"There's something different," Lisar insists. "I can see it in your eyes."

"I don't want to burden you with it." I sigh.

"Lyssy." Lisar grabs my hand. "It's me. We're in this together, remember? No secrets, no lies. That's not what marriage is."

"I saw my own death." It escapes from my mouth before I can stop it, out of my own control. I can't carry this burden around by myself one second longer.

"What!" Lisar yelps. It catches some attention. Bryn and Tomlien turn around; they continue on when Lisar waves his hand at them.

"Explain," he hisses. "What do you mean you saw your own death?"

"Baba Yaga gave me a potion that made me see the future, as a test to obtain the plants," I say. "In the vision I saw myself die as a result of being exposed to sunlight."

"Are you sure she wasn't trying to scare you?" Lisar's face is pale, his voice stretched and tight. "What else did you see?"

"Salkovia being attacked by witches, and my mother, with a baby." I bite my lip. "That's it.

Lisar's face strains. "Lyssy… your mother's dead."

I pause. "I know." I begin playing with a strand of loose hair, twirling it around my finger. "That's what doesn't make any sense."

Lisar shakes his head. "If the vision showed your mother then there's no possible way it could be true. Baba Yaga gave you that potion on purpose, to see if it would scare you away."

"If this is what's meant to be then we can't change it," I say firmly. "We will handle it when it comes to pass, and not before. We can't live our lives based on being scared of things that haven't arrived yet."

Lisar shrugs, though it's a nervous movement. "Whatever you say, Lyssy. But I know it's wrong. If you saw your mom then it's fake. The vision isn't real. There's just no way."

Lisar clenches even more tightly to my hand on the way back to the Jeep, like he's afraid if he releases his grip the future will come to pass at any moment. I don't let go, drawing comfort from the feel of his fingers wrapped in mine.

It eats away at me that I didn't tell Lisar the vision will only come to pass if I choose to marry him. But I promised myself that I wouldn't let any outside forces influence our relationship ever again, and I intend to keep that promise.

Could this be an exception to the rule? Probably. Doesn't change it.

I think more on the vision of my mother. She was so beautiful. Her eyes were like mine, hair, same length and color as mine. Even our red lips were the same. It was nearly like looking into a mirror—

It feels like a hammer hits me in the chest as a realization plummets into me. Perhaps I didn't see my mother. Maybe the vampire who was running was me.

But then, who is the baby?

SIXTEEN

*I*t's daylight when the plane lands at the Salkovian airport. Shioni brought enough sun lotion for us vampires to go around, so we smear it on and disembark the plane.

I wince when I step into daylight, remembering my vision. I expect my skin to start peeling off, but obviously, the sun lotion protects me. Lisar notices and puts an arm around me, drawing me to him as we walk to the snowmobiles. The others give me curious looks, though they don't say anything.

I hate this. I hate the reality of the sun. I want the safety of the night.

I cling to Lisar's back like a life raft as the snowmobile flies toward Salkovia. My eyes survey the tundra. They spot things a human eye would miss; flashes of red on the horizon, disappearing and reappearing. At first, I think I'm seeing things, until the red appears more than once. Those are cloaks. We're being followed.

Thankfully, nothing happens. We roll through Salkovia's gates unprovoked, and they slam shut behind us. Town is empty, as the other vampires are taking shelter from the day.

The others are in good spirits, but this worries me. If we were being tailed by witches just now, the only reason why they wouldn't attack us is to not blow their cover for a more important operative later.

Baba Yaga's words echo true. Many witches are about to die. I only wonder how many vampires and werewolves will join them.

"I'll start work on the remedy immediately," Shioni says, getting off her snowmobile at the entrance of the House of Antov. "I promise you I will not rest until this cure is completed."

Shioni tatters off, and Serghei follows. Rosa turns to the group and asks, "So what do we do now?"

"Now we wait," Lisar replies. "There's nothing else we can do."

"I can't sleep," Rosa moans. She's made a path in the snow, a circle from her pacing back and forth. "There's just no way."

"None of us can," Lisar replies.

"Hey Alpha, heads up!" A snowball comes whirling through the air and smacks against the side of Lisar's head.

"You little…" Lisar scoops up a pile of snow bigger than his head and chucks it at Georgie. The snowball lands in the middle of the boy's chest and knocks him flat out onto his back.

"Snowball fight!" Kipcha bellows, raising a fist over his head. He scoops up a snowball just as big as the one Lisar made with one hand and tosses it Rosa's way. It lands on her head. She sneers and chucks two tiny snowballs at Kipcha, that miss and hit Bryn.

She joins in, smacking everyone within an arm's throw with snowballs. Her snowballs are packed with ice, and hurt. Several wolves groan in pain as they make their impact, and Bryn smiles with each one.

While the wolves mess around, Tomlien, Elizaveta, Fyor, Valeri and I stand there like idiots, unsure of what to do. Wolves are playful, but a snowball fight isn't something a vampire would ever consider doing. It's too undignified. Childish.

Then a snowball from Bryn lands against Tomlien's shoulder and plops onto the snow. She freezes. She was aiming for Rosa. Tom is as still as a statue, unsure of what to do.

Then he stoops down, scoops up some snow and tosses it at Bryn. It lands on her leg. Bryn smiles a bit and throws another snowball back. Soon they're off in their own little world, a private snowball fight between the two of them.

Elizaveta winks at me. She makes a small snowball of her own and pitches it at Kipcha. When it hits him, Kipcha goes crazy. He tackles Elizaveta from behind, wrapping his arms around her middle and swinging her around. Elizaveta doesn't laugh, but her eyes sparkle.

At the sight of their commander caving, Valeri and Fyor join in. I follow suit, tossing a weak snowball at Lisar, which misses.

Out of the corner of my eye, I'm watching Bryn and Tom. Both of them are smiling for what seems like the first time in days. They're getting as close as they can without touching one another. Tom's got this weird look on his face. It's *so* obvious he's flirting. Lisar saunters over to me.

"For being broken up they sure don't act like it," Lisar says. He launches another snowball, which sacks Kipcha in the face.

"I know," I say. I throw a few more snowballs, but they're half-hearted, and they don't hit anybody. The snowball fight is fun, but there's something off about it. It feels… normal. I'm not used to it. I don't even know if I *like* it. How can we be playing like children when the witches are out there plotting something?

"It seems like everyone is getting along." Lisar's head turns as he watches Rosa and Valeri wrestle none too playfully, from Rosa smacking Valeri with a ball of ice on the side of the head on purpose. "Well, almost everyone."

Georgie and Fyor are tossing friendly little snowballs at each other and giggling, which is surprising due to Fyor's large stature. He could easily make a snowball that could knock Georgie out. I'm sure if Georgie had a tail he'd be wagging it.

Lisar forgoes snowballs and starts punching Kipcha playfully. He retaliates in kind, and soon the two of them are duelling in the square.

Elizaveta tugs on my arm. I hadn't noticed her sneak up behind me. She managed to get away from Kipcha while he and Lisar were tossing friendly punches at each other. Silently, we sneak away from the snowball fight and around a corner.

"You noticed the red cloaks too, didn't you?" I ask the question before she can explain. Nothing gets past Elizaveta.

She nods. "I'm leaving to put all the vampires on high alert. Can you tell Kipcha where I'm going?"

"Why can't you just tell him yourself?" I ask flatly.

She bites her lip. "I can't."

Her cloak sweeps behind her as she slips down the streets of Salkovia and to the barracks. Grumpily, I return to the group.

"Now where is she heading off to?" Lisar asks, thumbing at Elizaveta. I shrug. I don't have the energy to explain right now.

"I don't know, but she's damn gorgeous from the back," Kipcha says idolizingly. Lisar gives his beta a weird look.

I don't have time for this nonsense. Lisar notices the look on my face. He grabs my arm and says, "Come on. We're going inside."

I don't object. Lisar leads me inside the house, to our room. When the door snaps shut he turns to me. He's still got a hand on my arm.

"Lyssy. You're irritated." His scowl matches mine.

"I am not," I deny stubbornly.

"Yes, you are." Lisar spins me around and pins me against the wall. My breath hitches. He leans in close to my ear and whispers, "Tell me what's wrong."

"No."

"Lyssy," Lisar says, as a warning.

I take a deep breath. "I just don't understand why we can't grow up."

"You're mad that we had a *snowball fight?*" Lisar seems flabbergasted.

"Aren't we a little old for this?" My voice has a hiss; I try to suppress it, but that only makes the anger come out stronger. "Haven't we grown tired of childish games after all we've been through?"

"Lyssy, we're still just kids." Lisar releases me. He takes a step back. "It can't be blood and war all the time."

"If we're still kids then why are we getting married?" I ask harshly.

"That's not the—"

Lisar shakes his head. "Listen, it doesn't matter how old you are, everybody wants to have a little fun sometimes. We've all got a kid inside of us. Anyone who believes they're not immature is fooling themselves."

"It's got nothing to do with maturity." I cross my arms tightly around my body, though it's more of a hug than a sign of defiance. "It's got everything to do with the fact that life isn't all joy and roses."

"You're exploding for no reason! This isn't why you're upset. What happened with Baba Yaga still has you rattled," Lisar says.

His voice is calm. He comes closer to me. His presence is like a balm on my fury, softening it. "I'm telling you, it's not real. It's just a witch's trick. Believe me."

"You don't understand." This is when I shatter. I put my face in my hands. "It was so scary."

Lisar takes me in his arms. He rests his chin against the top of my head as he rocks me back and forth. "I know it was. But you can't believe it."

"How can I not believe it?" My voice is muffled against his chest.

"When have we been able to trust witches, huh?" Lisar shakes me. "We can trust Shioni, but that's only because she grew up with us, the pack. The rest of them are out to get us. Why would Baba Yaga want you to win? She claims she's impartial, but all the other witches are on Dragomir's side, so why wouldn't she be? Why wouldn't she want to scare you?"

I lift my head to gaze upward at him. "If that was true she wouldn't have given us the ingredients to turn you back."

"We don't know that. She could have all kinds of motives." Lisar's eyes are soft and kind. "Listen. Don't think about it anymore. It's the future, we don't know what it holds. It's pointless to worry about something we can't predict. We have other things to worry about." He smiles broadly. "Like wedding planning."

I release a sigh, letting it go. "I suppose you're right. Why worry? We have too much on our plate as it is."

He strokes my hair back. "Don't worry, Lyssy. I would never let anything like that happen to you anyhow. Nobody will ever be able to hurt you with me around."

Lisar starts to kiss me. It was meant to be a cute peck, but it quickly turns into so much more. I fumble with the zipper on his parka and then slide it off just before I rip off my own jacket and pull my shirt over my head. Right now, I need to feel comforted. I want to be loved.

"What are you doing?" he says breathily against my mouth as his hands move upward.

"I need you," I whisper back. I continue kissing him as the rest of our clothes are removed. We tumble onto the bed like a waterfall, roaring and unstoppable. Lisar uses one arm to flip me underneath him. He places hot kisses on my shoulder blades and neck, moving aside my hair and pressing into me. As his body moves over mine the horrifying images finally fade away and become fantasy, not reality.

Right now I just want to get lost in Lisar. Everything else is unimportant.

* * *

WE'RE STILL LYING NAKED in bed an hour later. I lie against Lisar's chest, tracing lines on his pectorals, while he fiddles with a strand of my hair. Cracks of sunlight filter past the dark curtains and onto the floor. It's just past noon. Neither one of us have moved, or said anything. Our eyes have closed, but it's like we're too exhausted to even sleep.

It's a testament to how tired we are.

A sudden explosion on the roof rattles both of us out of our stupor. It sounds like a bomb went off. Both of us jump at the sound. It's quiet for a few moments after, then smaller explosions follow, peppering the roof like tiny grenades.

"What's going on?" Lisar mumbles. He stops playing with my hair and sits up, blinking blearily.

"Hold on. I'll go check." I untangle myself from Lisar's arms and woefully pull myself from the warm sanctuary of the bed. I stumble to the corner, peering around the curtains and carefully avoiding the sunlight that pools from the window.

I gasp. Witches in red cloaks, hundreds of them, march through the streets of Salkovia with no force to oppose them. From their hands fireballs launch, landing on the rooftops of buildings and lighting them ablaze. A large hole has been blown in the walls, the gates lying broken into pieces at Salkovia's entrance. More and more witches flood into the town, doubling the amount of vampires that live here.

My vision. Already, it came true. The army of witches has arrived in broad daylight. Salkovia is defenseless, and completely unprepared. We vampires can't fight underneath the light of the sun, but neither can we remain in houses to be burned alive.

We're doomed.

SEVENTEEN

"*V*alentina's army is here." I get my unisex combat outfit out of the drawer and throw it on, tossing one to Lisar that I stole from the training arena that's his size.

He doesn't need to ask questions. He slips one the one-piece as I clip my pistols and dagger to my belt, then follows me out the door, if not a little sleepily. It's like he's used to all the chaos and doesn't question it anymore.

The first place I think to go is Shioni's room, but it seems everyone else already has the same idea. I walk into a full room of vampires and wolves, all of us armed with an array of blades and guns.

"We know," Serghei says as I open my mouth. "We're trying to do something about it."

"The potion isn't ready," Shioni says in a panic. She stirs the pot three times before adding something powdery in a bottle. Sweat has broken out at the top of her brow and her hair is a mess. "It still needs a few hours to brew."

"Of course she would attack us when we're at our weakest," Elizaveta says spitefully. "How are we supposed to fight during the day? There isn't enough sun lotion for all of us."

"This isn't for you. Valentina made a test for me," Shioni says darkly.

Shioni raises herself away from the potion. With her eyes toward the ceiling and palms lifted over her head the witch chants a strange spell, the words foreign and jilted to my ears.

When the incantation is complete, Shioni starts throwing up. She reaches for a cauldron and hurls into it, vomiting over and over again through her stomach is empty. Bryn launches to her side and puts her hands on her shoulders.

"What did you do?" I ask.

"I made… a cloud cover over Salkovia," Shioni whispers sickly. "No sunlight will be able to get through, but my magic has been spent resisting Valentina's power. She's attempting to break the spell, but she won't be able to as long as I remain conscious."

That doesn't seem promising. The young witch is wavering on the spot.

Elizaveta, the badass she is, decides to take that chance and says, "I'll mobilize every vampire we've got. We'll chase these witches out of the city. Serghei, come with me. I'll need you to command."

Serghei doesn't waste any time. His hand is on his *shahska*, gripping it tightly as if eager for battle. He and Elizaveta head for the barracks. The rest of us are left watching the witch curled up on the floor.

"I need help to finish the potion," Shioni whispers. "And protection."

"Count me!" Georgie offers. "I'll help."

"Me too," Rosa offers. She helps Bryn pick Shioni off the floor. She can barely stand; this isn't looking good.

"That makes three of us," Kipcha says valiantly. "We might not be able to change, but we can still fight. I can assure you there's no way in hell any witches are getting through that door."

"The rest of us will go out there and take down as many as we can," Bryn says viciously. She changes into a wolf before looking at Tomlien. "Right, Tommy?"

Tomlien seems momentarily shocked she addressed him, but he nods. He starts loading his rifle. Lisar nudges me and says, "Lyssy, give me your spare pistol."

"You can't change," I protest as I hand him the gun, a Ruger SR45. He pockets an extra box of bullets that I hand him as well.

"I'm standing beside you no matter what," he says. "Let's go."

The four of us hustle out of Shioni's room, through the main hall and to the doorway. No point in being stealthy; the witches are already here. Bryn slams her shoulder into the door, busting it open and flying onto the city streets. She springs upon a group of witches with her mouth open, ripping out the throat of her nearest prey.

Shioni's cloud cover is so effective that it appears almost night. I'm a little hesitant, but Tom isn't. He follows Bryn like he has no better place to be than with her. He slams the butt of his rifle against the head of a witch before impaling another with the bayonet attached to the barrel.

He doesn't burn. I stick out my arm as an experiment. When it doesn't sizzle, I point my pistol at the nearest witch and start firing, taking cover behind a fallen wall. Lisar joins me, both of us shooting off multiple rounds before being forced to reload.

It's slow, and clumsy. Guns are practically useless on witches. The bullets we shoot they're easily able to dissolve, or put up a shield against.

Fustrated, I chuck my pistol aside with a roar and spring over the wall with my dagger out. I dive it into the chest cavity of one witch before slicing open another. When they die, both witches turn to dust. They explode in a dusty demise, and ashes enter my eyes and mouth.

Temporarily blinded, I wipe at my face before moving onto the next witch. She goes to cast a spell, a blue ball forming in her right hand, but I slice it clean off. She clutches at her stump of a hand, screaming, before I silence her forever as my dagger slides through her mouth and comes out at the back of her throat.

Witches have spells, but if we can get to them before the magic can be casted, they can be defeated.

Bryn's being knocked back and forth in the air like a tennis ball between two witches, but as I slash their ankles she comes crashing back down to the ground. Both of us latch onto the witches, and they're done for.

Another witch shoots fireballs at Lisar. He hops from one foot to the other as the witch sends spells, toying with him.

Rage wells within my breast. I come from behind, grabbing the witch's arms and ripping them from her torso. She screams violently as her arms erupt into torches, the spell uncontrolled. I throw them at her and her entire body bursts into flames. I have to dodge to the side as the spell explodes, sending ashes and body parts spraying everywhere.

Tom's screaming from some invisible torture spell. A witch laughs as she hovers over him, twisting her hands until the veins in his hands and face begin to pop out.

I go to save him, but Bryn gets there before I do. She changes back into a girl and wraps her arms around the witch's head. With brute force, she pulls it right off. The witch's dismembered head hangs by a thread of flesh upon her neck, eyes wide open with shock, before she dissolves into a pile of ashes.

Lisar has abandoned the Ruger completely and is now using his bare hands. He picks up an abandoned sword a dead vampire dropped and uses it to spear witches through while they're casting a spell. Even without his powers, he's still formidable.

It's not long before I'm tripping over bodies, the snow red with blood. I notice something as we're battling; all of these witches are inexperienced, young. Some as young as sixteen. Valentina doesn't have all the witches on her side. The elderly ones, those with the most power, chose to stay out of this war. She could only manipulate the young into serving her.

It's a huge blessing. If Valentina had witches on her side that were as powerful as she, we wouldn't stand a chance.

Witches aren't the only ones dying. Vampire after vampire meets their end against the army of witches. I start to panic as I realize there are more dead vampires than witches. We're losing.

Then a trumpet sounds from behind. I whirl around to see a horde of vampires *riding polar bears*, lined up on top of a hill. All the vampires are carrying long spears in one hand, clenching the reins of bridles connected to the polar bear's heads. The polar bears are lashing their teeth, and look angry.

Serghei and Elizaveta are riding the largest polar bears. Serghei raises his spear, points it at the witches, and screams, "CHARGE!"

The polar bears barrel at the army of witches, and the vampires lower their spears. The witches go to run, but too late. The ones that aren't instantly impaled are bitted in half by the polar bears' huge jaws or are disemboweled by their gigantic claws. Many of them try to cast spells to stop the charge, but they aren't fast enough. Serghei's polar bear rears up and crushes several witches underneath him, while Elizaveta slides three witches at the same time onto her long spear.

The witches are no match for the polar bear army. "Fall back!" a witch screams. "Fall. Back!"

The army of witches scream bloody murder as they trample over each other to get out of the way. The polar bears begin to feast on limbs while their riders make quick work of the witches who are still alive.

Soon there's more ash in the area than snow. The Salkovians cheer as the witches retreat… what's left of them, anyway.

A nervous laugh escapes me. Thank Dracula for Elizaveta and her damn pets. Salkovia is safe. We've claimed victory. Valentina's army wasn't strong enough to defeat us like I feared. Even better, we've eliminated the threat. Valentina has no more army to command, no more cards to pull.

"Vampires riding polar bears," Lisar says in disbelief, watching the battalion as they chase the witches away. "Now I really have seen everything."

"Well, yeah! What's cooler and more powerful than a vampire riding a polar bear? Nothing!" Bryn squeals in excitement with a playful glance at Tom. He's still shaken from battle, but he manages to give her a shaken smile. Maybe the two of them are on their way to reconciling.

"All right guys," I say. "Let's regroup and see if Shioni is done with—"

A low growl sounds from behind me. It's a familiar growl, one I've come to hate… to despise.

A large black wolf prowls from around the edge of the city, unseen by the polar bears and vampires. His eyes are cloudy and red, jaws dripping with saliva.

Nicolae Lepescu. Lisar and Bryn's father. He's here.

"Hello, my children," he seethes. "Come to your senses yet?"

I launch myself forward to hold Lisar back before my Alpha can make a move. I catch him just before he springs, but he struggles against me to get to his father.

"Lyssy, let me go!" Lisar grunts as he pulls at my arms.

"Lisar, it's a trap! You can't fight him like this!" I say.

I can hold back Lisar, but not Bryn. She transforms back into a wolf, the hair raising up on her back.

"You killed my mother!" Bryn screams. It's a torturous scream, filled with vengeance and pain.

Nicolae snorts. "So I did," he rasps. "Are you foolish enough to meet the same fate, my daughter? Already, your love for the vampire has led you to a path of pain and suffering."

She raises her lips in a snarl. "I am no daughter of yours."

"I told you if we ever crossed paths again I'd kill you, Nicolae!" I bellow, still struggling to hold Lisar back. "Don't think I won't make good on that promise!"

"I don't care. The pack is gone," Nicolae spits. "We have nothing, *are* nothing. All there is left to do is take revenge on the ones who started it all."

I think that Bryn's going to attack first, but she doesn't; it's Tom. The vampire launches at him with his sword out, but Nicolae doesn't fight.

He flees. The wolf turns tail and starts sprinting in the opposite direction through town, leaping over bodies and debris. Bryn and Tom follow, chasing after the wolf without any thought.

Lisar stops fighting me, confused. I pause, just as mystified. Nicolae would never run. He would always stand and fight if it meant getting a chance at killing me.

Then I understand... the cloudiness in his red eyes... someone's enchanted him.

"Bryn, Tom, stop!" I scream, my throat ripping in half as I let Lisar go. "He's been bewitched!"

Neither one of them hear me. Lisar runs after them. We chase the couple through town, woefully behind. Our few seconds hesitance has cost us everything.

Bryn's ahead of Lisar and I, but Tomlien's faster. He catches up with Nicolae as the wolf is about to cross a bridge... Sorrow Bridge.

"Stop!" I cry. I trip and fall flat on my face, cutting the area above my eye. I ignore it and continue on, Lisar hustling to catch up.

Once on the bridge, Nicolae stops. He turns around and faces Tomlien with bared teeth, finally ready to fight.

"I'm going to kill you for the pain you've caused my dear Bryn-wolf," Tomlien says hatefully as he points his sword at Nicolae. "I will make you feel everything she felt, suffer through every heartache she endured. But for you, it'll be permanent."

Tomlien and Nicolae launch into battle. Tomlien lashes his sword out at the former Alpha, but Nicolae leaps or rolls to the side to avoid the blows, snarling.

Something is wrong. I know Nicolae's fighting style. He isn't trying to kill Tom. He's simply buying time.

"Tommy!" Bryn dashes onto the bridge beside him. Her hackles are raised as she skids next to her father and launches herself into attack. She and Nicolae roll over each other, tearing at one another with their teeth and aiming for the throat. Tommy circles the battle, looking for a place where he can get a hit in on Nicolae without hurting Bryn.

My eyes witness something terrible. Lidia is there, waiting on the other side of the bridge. Her hands are raised. They sparkle with a devious magic, eyes twinkling with a malice I've only witnessed before in Dragomir's eyes. She's just as crazy as he is.

"Like I said, Lysandra," Lidia yells across the void, "this is just the beginning!"

Lidia pulls down her hands with a sharp jerk, and the supports underneath the bridge collapse. Both edges of the bridge connecting to the land break and crumble downwards, falling down the ravine. All that's left of the bridge is the middle that Bryn, Tomlien and Nicolae stand on. It weaves on thin supports, about to snap in two.

Lisar starts screaming. Only now does Bryn recognize Lidia. Her claws grip the wood as the bridge begins to sway back and forth.

Tomlien's confused, looking down like he can't understand why the structure is suddenly collapsing. Nicolae laughs deliriously, consumed by the enchantment and unable to escape Lidia's command.

Bryn doesn't waste any time. She latches her teeth onto Tomlien's leg. The curse immediately takes hold, and her eyes contract. Viciously, she digs her fangs in.

Tom screams in pain, but Bryn is able to resist the curse long enough to toss Tomlien across the gap, to the embankment and to safety. Consumed by the curse, but unable to reach Tom, Bryn goes for the nearest thing within her reach... Nicolae.

At first, Nicolae fights. But as Bryn tears into him, he doesn't resist. The cloudiness leaves his eyes and the enchantment dissolves awy as Bryn rips her teeth into Nicolae's gut, disemboweling him. His organs slump out of the wound and onto the bridge.

She doesn't stop there. Bryn tears into his neck, ripping open the muscles and bursting the arteries. Nicolae is long dead, but she doesn't stop ripping his body to shreds.

As she continues the carnage the bridge continues to collapse, until the distance to land is too far for her to jump. Bryn cannot make the leap and hope to land on the other side. Perhaps a moment ago... but not now.

It was a sacrifice she knowingly made for Tomlien.

By the time the curse wears off, Bryn is covered in blood and Nicolae is little more than a pile of meat on the crumbling bridge. She doesn't appear sorry.

Lisar and I scamper beside Tom. We feverishly look for a way to get to Bryn as the bridge sways back and forth, but there's no way. The gap is too wide.

"Bryn!" Lisar reaches out his arms, as if hoping to catch his baby sister. "Bryn, come on, you can make it, come on!"

"BRYNWOLF!" Tomlien screams. Tears are pouring down his face like rain. Not since I was little have I seen him cry. He crawls to the edge of the cliff and bawls, watching Bryn sway back and forth on the bridge. Another support breaks, and she slides to the side.

I just kneel there stupidly, uselessly. I can't do anything. I already know what comes next. My eyes catch Lidia's across the way; they give a triumphant sparkle before she vanishes.

"I'm sorry, Tommy." Bryn's eyes are sad as she stares at the vampire she longed to be her mate, but could never be. "I love you."

The last support gives way. Lisar and Tomlien give bloodcurdling, traumatic screams as Bryn's body hurtles downward, tumbling through the air at a vicious speed and shattering on the rocky river below.

The acceleration of the fall makes her body and Nicolae's pierce the ice layering the top. There's the sound of bones shattering firing like gunshots through the air.

Bryn slips underwater with her father's body. The current sweeps her corpse away underneath the ice, never to be seen again.

EIGHTEEN

omlien's still screaming. And screaming. I shake him to get him to stop, but he won't. He's clawing at the edge of the ravine where Bryn fell, attempting to throw himself off of it after her. It takes all I have to pin him down.

Lisar doesn't do anything. He's slumped on his hands and knees, fists bunched up, face scrunched into a torturous expression of agony.

When he rises back up again, he sits back and watches me hold onto Tomlien vacantly. He doesn't cry. He doesn't shout. It's like there's nothing left in him anymore.

Everyone in his family is dead. He's the only one left.

"Alpha!" Georgie's panicky cry makes my gut sink even lower than I thought it could go. Kipcha, Rosa, and Georgie run toward us, tears on all their faces. They didn't see Bryn fall, which makes me instantly think of the potion. Something else is wrong.

"Alpha." Kipcha is breathless. Even his cheeks are wet. "I… we…"

He's too flustered to even speak, but his voice quiets as he notices Lisar, and me clutching Tom. His face turns pale white as an expression of utmost horror blooms on his face.

"Take us to Shioni," I say to them, any of them.

The moment I let go of Tom, Kipcha and Georgie take over. They have to lay on him to get him to stop resisting.

With difficulty, I haul Lisar to his feet. I have been doing this far too often. Instinct kicks in and he follows, or more or less stumbles after my lead. There's a problem, an issue. He's an Alpha. He can fix problems.

He can't fix death.

"Follow me," Rosa says. She leads the way as Georgie and Kipcha wrestle Tomlien to the ground. A bout of relief flows through me as I see Valeri and Fyor approach to help. It's going to take more than those two to get Tom under control. Right now, his entire world has ended.

We don't ask Rosa questions about what's going on. We don't have to; I've already guessed.

"I'm so sorry." Rosa's voice is regretful as we enter the House of Antov. It's an emotion I've never heard from her before. "Witches got in, we did our best but..."

She doesn't need to finish. The sight of Shioni kneeling on the floor is enough. She's covered in the potion that's spilled all over the floor. The cauldron is tipped upside down, still leaking out a trickle of fluid that smokes as it drips onto the cobblestone.

The cure. It's ruined. The wolves are trapped like this forever.

Shioni weeps into her hands loudly. Lisar sags against me; I have to reach out to catch him before he passes out and smacks his head on the floor.

I wonder if I did the right thing by holding Tomlien back.

We won today, but the price was so high to do so we may as well have lost.

* * *

It seems like everything's been frozen over since Bryn died.

When a pack member dies, the entire pack feels it. I am no exception. It seems cruel that the world continues to turn without Bryn here, that life goes on though she does not. We've lost all hope.

Her funeral was a few days ago. They searched for her body, but never found it; I knew they wouldn't. The ice is too thick, the river, too large. The water probably swept her body far away by the time we even started mobilizing people to look for her.

The ceremony was beautiful. Though he'd had to pause several times, Lisar gave a speech that made me cry.

"Bryn loved being a wolf, more than any of us," he'd said. "Even though we can't change anymore, we owe it to her to be the best wolves we can be. In her honor."

It's incredible how he's brought us all together after what's happened. I didn't know he could move people like that, but I guess that's the Alpha in him.

I watch the sun set over the horizon, leaning on the railing of an abandoned balcony off a vacant bedroom in the House of Antov. I came here to be alone; too many vampires have stopped by my bedroom to offer condolences lately, and even in the daytime, I can't sleep.

The sun is a round, red orb dipping beneath a flatland of snow, a world that doesn't change in one way or another. It's difficult to think there are other places on earth. Warm, safe places, places without the cold. All seems chilling now.

Lisar comes up behind me. He loops his arms around my waist and settles his chin against my shoulder, nestling his face into my hair.

"Your birthday's coming up," he says softly. "Only a few more days now."

"To be honest I've forgotten all about it," I respond. "It doesn't seem important now."

Lisar is silent for a moment. Then, "I was wondering if you still wanted to do it."

"What?"

"Marry me."

I turn to him. He keeps his arms firmly locked around me, hands settling on my lower back. "Of course I do. But are you saying we should still get married on my birthday, like we planned?"

"Yes."

Shock ripples through me. "It's only been a few weeks," I say gently. "Are you sure this is the right time?"

"We need some happiness to distract us from all this… stuff." Lisar sighs. His eyes are sad… old. I would do anything to make them happy again. "I can't figure anything that's happier than a wedding, can you?"

"I'd thought we'd postpone the wedding until a year after…" I can't bring myself to say Bryn's name.

Lisar shakes his head. "No. She wouldn't want us to wait. You know she'd want us to carry on without her."

I nod. "I suppose you're right. Should I tell Elizaveta to start making the arrangements?"

"Yes. That gives us a few days," Lisar says. "It's fine if it's a last-minute deal. I don't really feel like making this a huge, drawn out thing."

"Nor do I." I give him a loving kiss on the cheek. "I'll let her know immediately."

I go to find Elizaveta, but he holds me back.

"I was thinking, we both could use a vacation," Lisar adds. "Since Valentina's army isn't around anymore, I don't think Dragomir's going to make a move anytime soon. We should take advantage of it while we can and get a break. I was thinking of honeymooning in Italy."

"Italy?" The thought brings a ghost of a smile to my face. The first since Bryn died.

"Yeah. Someplace warm, sunny. Maybe Verona."

The notion seems wonderful. "A city of lovers. Yes, perfect. We'll be married, and leave for Verona shortly after."

I hug him tightly. He embraces me back, the muscles in his back hard and tense. I can feel them cease up beneath my fingertips.

"Hey, Lyssy?" he breathes. He takes a quick breath. "Don't leave me."

"Never." I kiss him on the lips tenderly, and don't bother to hurt him with the promise that it's going to be fine before going.

On the way downstairs, I run into his beta. Kipcha's face is dark and hollow as of late. I know he's going to get Lisar, and I know exactly where they're going.

"Kipcha!" I snag him by the back of the shirt. "You're taking him to the bar *again?*"

"Yeah," Kipcha says helplessly. "I don't know what else to do. Nothing helps him."

Lisar's been drinking far too much since Bryn passed. "Please don't. Lisar and I have decided we're still getting married," I say.

"You are?" his eyes widen. "Same day and everything?"

"Yes. Go plan the bachelor party, or something. He needs something to do," I say, giving him a gentle push.

Kipcha nods, and we part ways. It isn't long before I run into Elizaveta. It looks like she's been following Kipcha from a distance, but she doesn't mind that it's me who has found her. She peers around the corner and watches Kipcha as he disappears into the room upstairs.

"Hello, Lysandra." Her eyes only meet mine when Kipcha vanishes. "I was merely taking a stroll."

"It's okay. I know you care about him," I say. Elizaveta glances down and doesn't answer.

I decide to break the tension. "Lisar and I still want to get married on the twenty-first," I say. "Can you make that happen?"

"That's a spot of good news." A small breath whooshes out from Elizaveta's lips. "Very well. I'll tell the chef, and the servants, so they can start decorating the chapel."

"Excellent. I'll let Serghei know. I'd like him to walk me down the aisle." It seems like such a pretty thought, one that's so happy. A distant emotion from what everyone feels now.

"Indeed. That would be ideal." She curtsys to me. "It shall be done."

To spare her the embarrassment, I decide to leave first. She's still staring at the spot where Kipcha was. "Elizaveta?"

"Yes, csarina?"

I look over my shoulder. "Don't feel like you have to hide how you feel from Kipcha. It's not worth it."

Her face does not betray her, and I sigh. "We all need to love one another. While we still have time."

* * *

137

ON THE NIGHT of December 20 Lisar and I stand in the chapel with Elizaveta, in awe of the splendor around us. The pews have been decorated with red ribbons and green garlands that stretch along the aisle. The stained-glass windows, newly polished, sparkle brightly, each of them circled with large Christmas wreaths. White blossoming white poinsettias from the greenhouse stand in giant golden vases taller than I. White rose petals sit in baskets on the seat of the pews, ready to be sprinkled on the red rug just before I take my walk.

It's a perfect winter wedding. For having to rush the wedding planning, Elizaveta did a fantastic job.

I only wish Bryn was here to see her brother take his vows.

"Everything's ready," Elizaveta informs us. "The food is being prepared tonight, and the band will be ready for the reception. All you two will have to do is get dressed and say I do."

"It's absolutely gorgeous," I breathe. "You've really outdone yourself."

"I'll say," Lisar says, turning on the spot. "Sure is fit for a csarina."

The chapel doors echo as Georgie and Kipcha enter. It stuns me a little they're carrying guns. "What now?" I ask, tired.

"Oh, this," Kipcha says, raising his rifle. "It's just for the stag party. We're going hunting, see if we can catch a caribou. We can't change but we can still hunt, right?"

Lisar's eyes glimmer. Just a little bit, like they used to. He brings me to his side.

"Don't wait up for me, okay?" he asks, shaking me. "I'll be gone until the wedding. You'll need your rest for when you marry me tomorrow, because you can bet I'll be keeping you up all day afterwards."

The boys "*Oooh,*" while Elizaveta rolls her eyes. I blush and nudge his side.

"Go," I say, laughing. "It's breaking tradition for the bride and groom to see each other before the ceremony besides. Have fun."

"Oh, I will." Before he goes, he leans down to whisper in my ear. "I can't wait to marry you tomorrow."

My stomach squirms pleasantly. He kisses me on the cheek before gambling off with the boys. They hit each other and laugh on their way out. It makes me hopeful that things might get better.

"I have to go as well," Elizaveta tells me. "I have to make sure the cake will be here on time. Try to get some rest. You'll need to get up early for hair and makeup."

"Very well." I tilt my head to her. "Thank you, Elizaveta. For everything."

Elizaveta curtsies before hustling off. The ominous echo behind me when the doors shut signify I'm all alone. I turn again to take in all the magnificence.

I can't believe it. I'm getting married tomorrow.

A lone shape catches my eye, someone leaning against the organ. It appears I'm not truly alone. There's someone else in the chapel. A dark vampire looms in the shadows, taking in the beauty with a lost expression.

How long has he been standing there? Tomlien's been known to hover, but still...

"I can't help but feel jealous," he starts. "I'm trying to be happy for you, I just—"

Tomlien wipes at his eyes. I can't manage much more than a weak, "I'm so sorry, Tom."

"Sorry isn't going to bring her back," he says harshly. He brings his hand away from his eyes; where there was once pain there's now nothing but anger and revenge. "After you and Lisar are married, I'm going out there to look for Valentina and Lidia. If I have to lose my own life in the attempt to take theirs, so be it. Don't try to stop me."

Tomlien sweeps away. He punches a vase before he leaves; it slams against the floor, sending flowers scattering everywhere.

I pick it up and straighten out the flowers, but they're no longer pretty and perfect. They're messy, crushed, and a bit broken.

I decide it looks better that way and leave it.

I pass Shioni in the streets of Salkovia. She doesn't even notice me; she sways back and forth, holding a bottle of Russian vodka I'm sure she got from Serghei. The death of her beloved princess and her failure at keeping the cure safe has dismantled her completely. The witch is going stark mad.

She believes all of this is her fault. I don't think responsibility can be put on anyone except Lidia and Valentina.

After taking a brisk walk around Salkovia, I return to my room. Hanging on the closet door is my wedding dress, wrapped in a black bag so Lisar wouldn't see. Elizaveta picked out a poofy, gaudy ball gown that I don't like and isn't me.

But I don't care. It's not about the dress. It's about Lisar and I.

Suddenly and unexplainably, a heavy tiredness falls over me. It's not that late, but I can barely keep my eyes open. Elizaveta was right. I should get some sleep. Tomorrow is going to be a long night.

I literally drag my legs to the bed, feeling like my limbs weigh a ton. When I flop onto the mattress, my body sinks into it. I previously believed the mattress too hard, but now it's perfectly soft beneath me.

This feels strange. It's not like normal tiredness… it's groggy, and strange, like walking through a fog. My eyelids flutter once, twice. I struggle to keep myself awake, but cannot. I am no longer in control of my body. The tiredness has enslaved me.

I don't realize that the exhaustion is part of an enchantment until I see Lidia's blazing brown eyes hovering over me. Before I can hope to break the spell my body settles into a deep, dark sleep, one from which I cannot hope to escape.

NINETEEN

*T*he rattling of chains brings me back into the realm of the living. I open my eyes, slowly. The room comes slowly into focus... it's a small stone cell, nothing inside but a chamber pot and some old straw. I'm chained to the wall, my hands clamped over my head in shackles and my feet wrapped with chains. I can wiggle, but can't move.

A torch lights in the cell, revealing metal bars. On the other side of the bars is Lidia.

And she's wearing my wedding dress.

I scream with fury. I pull myself against the shackles, which cut into my wrists and ankles. They don't budge. The very wall should've given way under my strength, but though I gnash my teeth and pull with all my might I can't get them to unleash. Not even a vampire's strength can break these chains.

"It won't do you any good," she says. "The spell's too strong."

"Lidia! Let me go!" I bellow; my voice echoes against the walls. "Take my wedding dress off!"

"I can't do that. I need it for when I'm pretending to be you," she responds.

"What do you mean?" My eyes narrow. I stop pulling against the chains to listen; there must be another way out of here.

"Don't you understand? This is what we've been planning all along." Lidia's voice is high-pitched and excited, like a little child's. "This is the best Christmas present ever. I get to be *you* for a day."

"Quit speaking in riddles and have it over with."

"The army was just a distraction, meant to weaken your forces and get you to let your guard down," Lidia says coolly. She doesn't like that I'm not playing along. "This is the main event. While you're locked up in here, I get to play house with the wolf."

Lidia waves a hand over her head. A spell emerges from her fingers and trickles downward, wrapping itself around her body like a tendril mist.

When the mist clears I find Lidia's dark hair changed to blonde, her brown eyes to blue. Her nose, cheekbones, facial structure are all mine. Her hands and feet are mine. I'm looking at an exact copy of myself, a twin in my own wedding gown.

"No," I say, breathless as I realize what she's doing. "No, no, *no!*"

"Oh yes, darling Lisar, I do, I do!" Lidia says, fluttering her eyelashes and mocking me. When she speaks, it sounds just like my own voice. *I* wouldn't even be able to tell the difference.

When she smiles, though, I see her plainly. I would never smile like that, so evilly and full of hate. I notice the difference. And Lisar will, too. He must.

"This is so much fun! I get to marry your wolf prince!" Lidia shrieks. "Then once the vows are said and the wedding is over, Valentina and I are going to slaughter everyone around! It's going to be amazing!"

Lidia waves her hand again. She changes back into herself, grinning like the Cheshire cat.

"The best part of it is nobody will realize that it's me. They'll all think *you're* doing this." Lidia sighs happily. "Finally, everyone is going to see that you're not so special after all."

"Why do you hate me so damn much?" I snarl. "I never did anything to you!"

"Never did anything to me?" Lidia's eyes flash. "Vampires captured my family and forced them to serve the Romanov line! Every human

I've ever known has been nothing but food, and breeding stock for your kind! My parents *died* serving Dragomir! I was forced to be your maidservant all my life, until I wised up and realized that I didn't have to anymore!"

"I'm not like my father!" I yell. "I was planning on setting the humans free when I became csarina!"

"Yes, but you did nothing in the meantime," Lidia responds coldly. "You watched as we were fed on and kicked around and tortured, and turned your gaze away."

"What could I have done?" I plead. "My father ruled over everyone, what choice did I have but to accept it?"

"You could've stood up to them!" Lidia bursts. "You could've said something, objected somehow, but you never did! You were too concerned with training and parties and dresses and whatever else was in your stupid little head at the time. You didn't care about what Dragomir did to others until Dragomir came for you!"

The most painful, shameful reality of the situation hits. She's completely right. I had responsibility and power as a ruler, and I let her people down. I allowed Dragomir to farm the humans like cattle with little objection.

I hang my head. "I'm sorry, Lidia. I should've done something."

"Yes. You should've." Lidia rises up. She takes a deep breath. "But it's okay. Once Dragomir gives Valentina our witch kingdom, we'll turn against him and set the humans free. She promised me. We're going to overthrow him together."

"You know Valentina will never let that happen. I'm sorry that I hurt you, but she's leading you on, Lidia."

"We'll see. Apologies won't save your skin now, or your wolf's," she says flatly. "I'm long past extending forgiveness."

"You were my best friend."

Lidia's hardened expression doesn't change. "I thought you were my friend, too. Until I realized we were different. That no matter what, I'd never be on your level. That's when I decided I no longer wanted to serve beneath you, but rise above, and become something more powerful than even you. Valentina saw the potential in me."

She grins wickedly again. "But now I'll have my revenge. I'll finally be able to destroy the wolf that tore us apart. Killing him is going to be so much fun."

"I don't care what you do to me, but leave Lisar alone!" I threaten. "I swear, if you touch him there won't be a hole you can crawl into where I won't find you, Lidia!"

"He's only slept with *you*, hasn't he? How cute," Lidia says gleefully, ignoring my last comment. "I'll make sure to fuck him before I kill him, just to spite you."

A flush rises up all over my body. Jealousy. Hate. Both are replaced by an irresistible urge to slaughter Lidia. I long to rip her body into a million pieces.

"He won't touch you," I growl underneath my breath. "He'll be able to see right through you. I know it. He'll realize it's not me."

"I don't think so. I can hear him now just before I yank out his heart. '*Lysandra, why did you betray me?*'" Lidia cackles.

"If you knew anything about us you'd know he's never called me by my full name," I snarl. "But you've never been in love, have you, Lidia? No man on earth would be crazy enough to love you."

"Tom would've loved me," Lidia says quickly. "He might love me still. He just doesn't know it. He'll come to his senses once he realizes you're gone."

"It's why you killed Bryn, isn't it?" I say, unable to stop myself. "You couldn't stand that she had his heart and you didn't."

"She doesn't matter," Lidia snaps. "He would've picked me."

"No. He always belonged to Bryn. Fate determined it," I whisper.

"SHUT UP!" Lidia's shaking; I've finally gotten to her. She bunches the skirt of my wedding dress into her fists as she shouts, "I'm going to marry the wolf you love, and there's nothing you can do about it!"

"Like hell you are! I should've murdered you that day in the tent." My fangs descend; I'm not playing around.

"But you didn't." Lidia's voice is so cocky, so arrogant, it only fuels my fury. "And now you're going to pay the price for your pity."

"It was never pity, Lidia." I shake my head. "It was mercy. But you better believe you're not going to get it from me a second time."

"I don't see you getting out of those chains anytime soon," she says, crossing her arms. "Have fun thinking about me on top of your fiancé."

"That's enough, Lidia." Valentina's cool voice emerges behind her apprentice's. She holds herself upright, regarding me coldly. "We have to leave."

"Why do you do this? This is unnecessary," I say to Valentina. "You could kill all of us without these dramatic theatrics. It's a bit over the top, don't you think?"

"It is what I promised Lidia. She deserves a moment in the spotlight after so many years of living in your shadow," Valentina says. "After what's done is done you will go back to your father. And this time, you won't escape."

Valentina pointedly looks at Lidia. She wiggles her fingers and says, "See you soon, Lysandra. I'll bring back some cake."

She and Valentina vanish. A guttural, animalistic scream emerges from my gut. It tears my throat. It shakes the walls. It defines my pain.

But it does not set me free. I yank at the shackles for a few more minutes before exhaustion overtakes me. This isn't getting me anywhere, this wild behavior. I need to calm down. I need to think.

One thing's for sure. I'm not gonna sit here and wait for Lidia and Valentina to kill everyone at my own wedding. I have to get out of here and stop them.

Then the cell door swings open. As it does, the shackles around my ankles disappear and the chains vanish. The entire cell was enchanted on the inside; now exposed to the outside world, the spell collapses completely. I'm free.

I'm about to breathe a thank you to my savior, before I look up and my entire body turns to ice.

It's Bryn.

TWENTY

"Oh my God. Bryn." I dart forward and cling her to me, shocked when her body connects against mine. She's not a ghost or an illusion, like I thought. She's solid, and though she's skinnier than she was before, she's really here.

I can't help but cry. It's been a terrible few weeks with Bryn gone. All the light went out of the world, and now it's back again. It's like I'm hugging someone that's not real. This feels like a dream. "You're alive!"

"Barely," she whispers. She starts wiping the tears from my eyes. "Don't cry, Lyss. I'm all right."

I pull away and look her over; she doesn't appear injured in any way. It definitely doesn't look like she plummeted thousands of feet through the air and landed on a sheet of ice a few feet thick.

"How did you survive?" I ask, gaping. "There's no way that fall didn't kill you."

"It did," she says quickly. "Well, not really. I don't remember much of the fall. I passed out before I hit, and woke up under the water. I was in so much pain. All my limbs were broken. I couldn't move, couldn't swim. I knew I was going to die. I didn't have long."

She sighs. "Then I felt someone pull me from the water. It was Valentina."

"Why would Valentina rescue you?" I say, astonished.

"I'm getting to that," Bryn says impatiently. "Lidia wanted to let me die, but Valentina was mad at her for using Nicolae as bait. Apparently he was a useful tool, good at giving out information."

"Did he tell Dragomir where the other packs are located?" I ask, chest filling with dread.

"Yes. But as far as I know, Dragomir hasn't made a move on them yet. He's been too busy trying to get at you," Bryn says. "Once he crushes the rebellion you've made there's no one to stop him from tearing the packs apart, so they're on the backburner while he deals with this."

"That still doesn't explain why Valentina saved—"

"Valentina thought Lidia wasted Nicolae's potential as a way to get at me." Bryn's nose crinkles. "They still needed a wolf informant, a member of pack hierarchy. With Nicolae gone and Lisar out of reach, I became the only candidate."

"So she saved your life?"

Her lip curls. "I hate to give her credit, but yes. She healed my body, mended all my bones back together and recrafted my organs. She thought she could put me in Nicolae's place and brainwash me, too."

Bryn shrugs. "Unfortunately for her, you can't be cursed twice. No matter what she did, it wasn't possible for her to undo the spell she already put on me, to keep Tommy and I apart. So she chained me up until she could figure out a way to eliminate her own spell."

"How did you escape?"

Bryn smirks. "How else? Stupid Lidia. I was in my human form when Valentina healed me. Had to be, see, to mend the bones. God, the magic was terribly painful. After it was done Lidia chained me up, but she didn't have the common sense to put an enchantment on me so I couldn't change. I turned into a wolf, the cuffs slipped off and I was able to squeeze through the bars. They've been going mad for days trying to find me."

"I'm surprised they haven't," I say.

"This place is gigantic," she says. "There are plenty of places for me to hide without even their magic locating me."

She frowns. "Though I haven't quite been able to escape yet. Tell me, is Tommy all right? And my brother?"

"They're both a mess, but they won't be once we get you home," I say. "What is this place?"

"It's a castle on the edge of The Sein, near Paris," she informs me. "Yes, France," she adds when my mouth drops. "I've learned that much since I've been here."

"We're so far away!" I moan. "We'll never be able to get to the wedding in time to stop them!"

"Yes, we will," Bryn says firmly. "There's an enchanted mirror, one Valentina keeps at the edge of the castle. It'll show you anything you want to see, or take you anywhere in the world you want to go. I think it's how Valentina has been able to find out where we were going and how she managed to get there quicker than us every time. You don't have to be a witch to use it. Just tell it where you need to go, then step inside."

"Why haven't you used it yet to get home?"

"Because it's not as easy as it sounds." She sighs again and turns around. "You'll see when we get there. For now, there's no time to waste."

I decide now isn't the time for questions and follow Bryn. We slip out the cell, and I look around. Hundreds upon hundreds of cells, stacked one top of the other, line the walls. The room is circular, several stories tall. Bryn and I start climbing the winding staircase upward. By the time we've climbed ten flights, I'm out of breath.

"The exit seems no closer than it was when we started," I remark, gasping.

"It isn't" Bryn says. "The staircase is stretching."

"What?" I ask. I look up and find with horror that it is; each step we take, the staircase only grows, adding steps and twisting higher and higher. Have we moved anywhere at all?

"Just keep going," Bryn says. "It'll appear eventually."

I don't know what Bryn means, but suddenly one of the cells vanishes and there appears a door.

When her hand touches the knob the door shrieks and laughs, but Bryn pushes it open without flinching and steps through.

"The castle is meant to confuse those who aren't witches," Bryn says. "Believe me. I've been trying to solve the puzzle for weeks and I'm just now getting the hang of it."

The door leads to a hallway. The hallway seems very long, but it only takes three or so steps before we're at the edge again. Bryn opens that door, which leads to another room, and then another and another until I'm quite dizzy. It feels like we're walking on the ceiling instead of the floor.

Finally, the next door that opens reveals an open foyer. My jaw drops. Above and below me are hundreds of flights, all with different staircases that appear and reappear next to random doors. Both directions seem to go on forever. Where one door vanishes, another appears. Stained glass windows and paintings in frames dance around each other, switching spaces. Carpets inch along the floor. Furniture gets up and waddles to one place, settling down just to get up and walk over to another moments later. The only thing that doesn't move is the stone beneath our feet.

"Witches purposefully made it so the doors rotate and the rooms reorganize, so that they're never in the same spot," Bryn says. "I swear I've found the main entrance three times, only to exit out the grand doors and find myself in the kitchens, or the ballroom."

"This place is gigantic," I whisper. "At least three times larger than Castel de Sange." You could fit hundreds, maybe even a thousand witches in here and they would never know anyone else was here at all by all the movement the rooms make. I can see why Bryn can't just walk out the front door. This place is a maze.

"I wonder what the history of this place is," I whisper. "This can't all be Valentina's work. It would take her years to craft."

"It's not. It's the spells of many witches over several centuries," Bryn says. "Each of the four main covens lived here in unity, but after humans grew distrustful of witches, they began to separate. The castle was abandoned shortly after Vlad Dracula rose to power. Witches went to work for vampires and werewolves who were already in hiding."

"But why? Why serve us?" I ask.

Before it vanishes, Bryn jumps on a staircase. I follow her lead and we vanish with it, appearing in a section of the castle I haven't yet seen, a large and open space. This must be the great hall.

"It was safer for them to hide instead of staying here, considering the witch hunts that were going on in Europe at the time," Bryn explains. "Still, I think they should've stayed and fought. This is impressive."

"How do you know so much about it?"

"I've been investigating where I can. Not much else to do besides try to find a way out."

Suspicion crosses my mind. I can't tell if something feels off, or if I'm still so shocked that Bryn is alive I just can't believe it.

"How do I know you're real?" I ask in an accusatory tone. "How can I be sure that you're really Bryn, and not some enchantment Valentina sent to fool me?"

"Of course I'm Bryn," she says irritably. "Why wouldn't I be?"

"I don't know that for certain," I say. My hand would be on my dagger if I had one.

"When I show you the mirror you'll know it's me, for real," Bryn says. "Just trust me, okay?"

I let out an anxious huff. "Fine." I don't have a choice, anyway. There's no way I can find my way out of here by myself. If she's leading me into a trap, at least she's leading me somewhere.

When we get off the staircase we find ourselves at the edge of a great divide. A giant stone bridge, broken into two pieces, hovers over a pit that you can't see the bottom of. The side where we are standing on leads back to a staircase, the other side connecting to the other half of a drawbridge. It brings me back to Sorrow Bridge. I flinch, but Bryn doesn't bat an eye.

Hovering in the middle of the bridge, suspended by magic, is a large silver mirror. It's Victorian in style, with floral flairs and brass adornments.

Something is off about that mirror. It's sinister. Cunning. I get the feeling it's smarter than me.

The reflective surface of the mirror shimmers. I look at Bryn expectantly, and she says, "Just watch."

Bryn walks to the edge of the bridge in front of the mirror. I feel so nervous that she's standing where she could fall off again that I want to rip her back, but I hesitate.

Bryn stares into her own reflection. Dread haunts her face, like she's about to see the living dead.

Then, in a clear voice, she says, "We wish to use the mirror."

The mirror gleams. At first it merely sparkles, but then light and an array of color beams from the surface. Bryn bites her lip and turns away, unable to look as the mirror bends and twists into the shape of a person.

Brass and silver becomes a dress of red silk and a fur cloak, the mirror shaping into a face. My hand flies to my mouth and I gasp as tears rise to my eyes for the second time that day. Long dark hair and a kind smile graces fair skin.

In place of the mirror and floating between the divide of the bridge is Sylvia Lepescu.

TWENTY-ONE

*B*ryn is staring at Sylvia with a lonesome expression in her brown eyes. My friend's face looks lost, innocent, almost like a child's. It's as if Bryn is a pup again, Sylvia stares down at her kindly, a motherly smile on her face.

"What's going on?" I ask quietly. Sylvia doesn't look at me when I speak.

"The mirror only shows our deepest insecurities and fears. That's what I figured out, anyway," Bryn says quietly. "You can't use the mirror unless you conquer what you're afraid of. Lidia always had to talk to you. Valentina always sees herself."

"How did they get them to move?" I ask.

"Lidia just gloated about how she was going to beat you. I got the feeling Valentina was frightened of her own power." Bryn doesn't take her eyes off Sylvia's. "She was able to talk herself aside. It doesn't matter which way, so long as you confront them."

"But you can't."

"No." Bryn shakes her head. "I've tried and tried, but I don't have the strength."

I walk behind Bryn. I grab her hand, and hold it tightly. "We'll do it together," I say. I give her fingers an encouraging squeeze. "As sisters."

Bryn's smile is ghostly. "Yeah. You're going to be part of this family. I guess this is how it starts."

As I approach the mirror, another figure appears next to Slyvia. She floats upon the air, her hair fair and white, lips redder than a rose, and skin paler than the snow upon the tundra. I wince when her icy eyes turn upon me.

"By Fane," Bryn gasps. "She looks so much like you."

"I know." I swallow heavily. Katya's stare is blank and vacant upon her hollow face. Her lips do not form into a loving smile like Sylvia's, but remain thin. She looks like she's starving from the inside out. I try to remind myself this is the mirror's representation of my mother, and not the real thing, but it only makes me feel worse. Is this how I remember her? Cold and distant?

I haven't seen her in so long that I can't describe the emotions that run through me. I want to leap off the bridge and into her arms, but I know it's a futile thought. She's merely an illusion.

"Hello, Mother," I say softly. "Will you let us pass?"

When my mother makes no attempt to respond, a sob rises out of my chest. She coldly watches as I crumble to my knees on the floor, unable to meet her gaze.

"Why are you doing this to me?" I ask the mirror. "This is torture!"

"Lyss! Snap out of it!" Bryn stoops down, hooks me by the elbows and drags me upward, back on my feet. "I had the same reaction, but we don't have time for this! Lisar is in trouble!"

"We aren't going to make it to my wedding!" I put my face in my hands and suppress tears as Katya watches. "He's going to end up marrying Lidia! My lord, Bryn, I'm going to lose him!"

"Not if we have something to say about it!" Bryn starts shaking me. "Pull yourself together!"

When I don't calm down, Bryn smacks me lightly across the face. I take some deep breaths to soothe myself. Bryn lets me go, but still watches me out of the corner of her eye.

"Right," I say shakily. I turn back to Katya; her gaze is as haunting as ever. "What do we say to get the mirror to let us pass?"

Bryn sighs. "This is the part where I'm stuck. No matter what I say,

Mom won't let me through. I've tried everything, told her I'm sorry I let her die, that it wasn't her fault, that I apologize for being so harsh to everyone since she died…"

"Maybe the mirror doesn't want apologies," I say. "Maybe it just wants you to be honest."

"I don't want to be honest," she mumbles. "It would be mean."

"Mean or not, it's how you feel. Think of Lisar," I say. "If that's not enough, do it for Tom. He wouldn't judge you for it."

Bryn nods slowly. "Okay. I'll give it a shot. For Tommy."

Bryn faces her mother again. She doesn't quiver, or appear to lose her mind, like I did. Bryn must've done this so many times now, in an attempt to get back to us. For weeks, this was her own personal hell. I'm not sure I could do it.

"Mom. There's some stuff I wanna tell you." Bryn takes a deep breath. "I just want to let you know I'm upset. I'm mad because I feel like you hurt me, and that you don't care."

Bryn started off polite. But now, her voice rises with each word. "I know you're gone and that I should remember the good times, but that doesn't make the pain go away. We lost everything… the home, the den, the pack… all because of you. You were selfish and tried to save Vasile instead of doing the right thing and letting him go for the sake of all of us."

Bryn's voice is very loud now. It's nearly screaming. "You chose your brother over your own damn kids. You put us in danger and ruined everything because he was more important than us. None of this would've happened if you'd just forgotten about Vasile, and put the pack ahead— no, forget the pack, just Lisar and me! Weren't we enough for you? Weren't we enough to make you forget about him?"

Bryn turns around. Sylvia's eyes are still on her as she takes a few steps away, then faces her mother once more. "You didn't do anything to stop Nicolae. You let him do whatever he wanted to us without saying *anything*. You weren't there. You betrayed the family, betrayed your own kids—"

Bryn stops to take a shuddering gasp. "I'm so *angry* at you, Mom. I'm angry you weren't there. I guess you did your best, but your best wasn't good enough, don't you understand? If it was, you'd still be here. You wouldn't have let Nicolae win. You would've stopped him."

Bryn's voice stutters as she says, "If you really cared you wouldn't have died."

The young she-wolf's breathing is harsh and labored. A single tear slips down her cheek. Sylvia reaches out with one finger and wipes it away before giving Bryn a smile.

Then she fades away.

Bryn gapes. She looks at the empty spot where her mother once was, then back to me, whispering, "It worked."

"It did." I nod to Bryn. The things she said to Sylvia didn't surprise me, although I don't agree with all of them; despite her many faults Sylvia was an adoring parent, fiercely protective of Bryn and Lisar. If she was strong enough she would've defeated Nicolae to save them. She just wasn't.

But regardless of whether it is the real truth, it is Bryn's truth. And it's something that had to surface for her to move on.

When Bryn stares expectantly at me, I realize we're only halfway done. We won't be able to get through if I don't convince Katya to stand aside.

"Your turn," Bryn says. She looks like she's worn out. "I'm right behind you."

I look at Katya. I'm not even really sure what to say. My emotions over my mother are so mixed up and convoluted. I'm not certain what's all there.

The mirror wants me to be honest. For me, I'm not sure what that means. But I decide to let what I feel lead the way.

"Hello, Mother," I say gently. She blinks at me. "It's strange, speaking to you like this after all these years. I never thought I'd see you again. Even though it's not really you."

My voice is so hollow. No change. I swallow and continue on. "I know you did your best... or at least, the best you could do. There were other things you could've done that would've made it better, but I don't think you thought about the options. You were too far gone by then to even realize you could've intervened."

This is the hard part. Like any of this is easy. "But what I want to know is *why*. Both of us suffered under Dragomir, not just you. You acted like it was only you who was miserable, but I was, too. You were my light, my one happy place in that darkness, and you took yourself away. I knew you could fight; you were an excellent warrior. You could've easily taken down those wolves, but instead you let them kill you. It was murder, but I think you still had a choice."

Bryn moves forward. She goes to put a hand on my shoulder, but at the last minute she draws away.

My voice wobbles. "I needed you! You gave up! You were so depressed and so self-centered that you forgot I was there! Why didn't you take me with you? We could've run away together. I don't know if we could've gotten far, but at least we could've tried! Why did you abandon me? Wasn't I good enough for you? Did I do something wrong? What was so terrible that made you not want to fight for me?"

"You didn't do anything wrong, Lyss," Bryn echoes sadly.

"Even worse, you made me watch you die, and it was terrible," I gasp. "I'll never forget a moment of it as long as I live. I hate you for that, but even worse, I love you too much to get over you."

I put a hand over my quivering lips. Unlike Sylvia, Katya doesn't reach out a hand, or another gesture of comfort.

She merely stares at me, blinks twice, and then goes away.

With her disappearance, the mirror reappears. It hovers downward at eye level, right on the edge of the bridge. The reflective surface of the mirror changes until it's a swirling pool of blue, purple and green colors.

"You did it, Lyss," Bryn whispers. She steps beside me. "You got the portal to work."

My lungs feel like they're on fire. I'm still recuperating from the absence of my mother. Though I was yelling at her, I wanted her here more than anything. Those few precious seconds with her were maddening, but they were all I had. Now I have nothing left of her.

With a hardened voice, I tell the mirror, "Take us to Salkovia. Siberia, Russia."

The mirror flashes. Colors beam out and shine from within the mirror, wrapping us in a magnificent stream.

I feel the familiar linkage of Bryn's fingers in mine. "Come on, Lyss," she says softly. "We've got to stop that wedding."

I nod, clenching my sister's hand tightly as if she's the only thing I have left to hold onto in the world. No one else shared this with me; not Lisar, not my grandfather. This secret moment between us, where we shared our deepest pain over our lost mothers, will bond us together forever.

Together, Bryn and I take a step through the mirror's portal and to Salkovia.

TWENTY-TWO

*T*he portal isn't rushing, or fast, or a swirling tunnel like I thought it would be. One minute we're at the castle, and the next, we're on the outskirts of Salkovia right outside the chapel.

I go to dive in right away, but Bryn grabs my wrist. "Wait!" She points to a thick trail of blood upon the snow, one that leads around the church.

The smell is familiar. Something horrible clicks in my head. "Serghei."

We follow the blood trail to the back of the chapel, where it ends at a small shed. There's a lock on it. Bryn starts looking for a key, but I'm so pissed that I just grab the thing and wrench it off with my bare hands.

"Nice," Bryn says. She pushes open the door. I gasp when I recognize Serghei on the ground, tied up and unmoving. He's bleeding from multiple cut wounds on his legs and chest. Relief blossoms in my chest when he opens his eyes.

"Grandfather." Bryn and I start forward and begin untying the rope. It's been enchanted, but the rope loosens when we touch it, as it wasn't us the curse was meant to hold.

"Thank goodness you girls came along," he says as the ropes fall away, rubbing his wrists. Serghei gives a strange look to Bryn, but other than that, shows no further surprise that she's alive. Do people frequently come back to life in war?

"Grandfather, Lidia is in disguise! She's going to marry Lisar instead of me!" I say.

"I already know, my dear. I was worried as to what they had done to you," Serghei says.

"We'll explain later. Why did they keep you alive?" Bryn questions as Serghei stands gingerly, letting out a moan. The poor vampire is getting so old.

"Dragomir wanted to deal with me personally," he says, cracking his knuckles. "I'm glad he won't be able to get the chance."

"Let's kick some ass," Bryn growls. She changes into a wolf and barrels out the shed door. Serghei and I follow. We're going in without weapons, but there's no time to waste. I'll claw their eyes out with my nails if I have to.

Serghei, Bryn, and I head around the chapel and to the front doors. Throguh them, I can hear Elizaveta say, "If anyone is to object to this union, speak now, or forever hold your peace."

I literally kick the doors down, stride into the church and scream, "I object, because that's not the damn bride!"

The crowd gasps, and all the attendees stand. There are several screams of shock. I can only imagine what a sight it is; the three of us dirty, one bloodied, one back from the dea, and me in particular looking like I'm half mad. Kipcha, Rosa, and Georgie's eyes pop out of their sockets. Elizaveta's mouth is open mid-sentence, and Fyor and Valeri choke.

Even Shioni, who appears slightly intoxicated, freezes.

Lidia's face, disguised as my own, twists into a nasty snarl. She quickly rights it before anyone else sees. She's adorned in my wedding gown, hair in a fancy updo I would never choose. I can't wait to get my hands on her. Valentina, disguised as Serghei, stands cooly at Lidia's side, eyes burning with anger.

Lisar makes a choked, strangled noise I've never heard him make in his life. His head flips from one Lysandra to the other, unsure of which one is his.

For a second, I lose sight of what's going on. He looks so stunning in a tux and bowtie, all the part of the groom I imagined he would be. He looks completely perfect in that moment, and I hate Lidia for tearing the special gift of walking down the aisle toward him away from me. My whole world centers and focuses on him, locked within his gorgeous stare.

When he catches sight of Bryn, however, I snap out of it. Lisar's eyes contract. His eyes well with tears as he cries, "Bryn, you're alive!"

Lisar starts forward to embrace her, but Lidia starts screeching. "Lisar, don't! It's a trap!"

She reaches out to grab Lisar, to hold him back. The sight of her hands on him infuriates me. I take a step forward but Serghei flings out a hand, to hold her back. The other Serghei merely raises an eyebrow, playing the part.

Valentina won't crack. It's up to Lidia to slip.

"Brynwolf." Tomlien stands from his place in the pews. He grips the wood so tightly his fingers blanch. His whole body seems weak as tears slip down his face. He's dying to touch her, but scared to. "Is it really you?"

"Oh, Tommy." Bryn's legs are quivering. "I missed you, Tommy."

"This is nonsense." Valentina speaks. She moves front of Lisar as the faux Serghei. "These are obviously imposters sent by Valentina. We must deal with them quickly."

"We're not imposters, they are!" I say, pointing a finger at the other me. "*They're* Valentina and Lidia! Lisar, I promise you that it's me!"

"Don't listen to her! I'm the real Lysandra!" Lidia croons. She strokes Lisar's arm gently. "Don't you believe me?"

"Lisar, smell her! You should be able to tell by her scent it's not her!" Bryn says angrily, stomping a paw.

"I... I can't tell. I don't have my powers." Lisar gulps.

"You had the potion when I left! What did you guys mess up now?" Bryn grumbles under her breath. I wave at her, to get her to shut up.

"Lisar, baby, you can't tell me you believe her," Lidia says. "You should be able to tell who the real me is."

Lisar stares at her. He slowly pulls his arm out of her grasp. "You have been acting weird all night…"

A smug smile appears on my face. Lisar notices, and my stomach drops as he says, "But that doesn't mean I believe you, either. Someone is lying."

Lisar looks at Shioni and nods. Now sober as a bird, Shioni steps forward and raises her hands over Lidia and Valentina, her hands glowing with an immense power.

Before Shioni can cast the truth spell, Valentina pushes her out of the way and runs for the door. Shioni falls, and the magic from her hands blasts upward, uncontrolled. It smacks Lidia right on the face, glowing outward like the sun. The enchantment melts away at my features until Lidia is standing there in my wedding dress, the updo sagging around her face and tendrils of hair sticking to her cheeks.

"Get away from me!" Lisar shouts, disgusted. He pushes Lidia roughly aside and she tumbles to the floor.

Valentina is still on the run, but Tomlien gets to her first. He grabs her ankle and pulls her down. As he does so, the enchantment fades until the witch resembles herself again. She snarls, kicking Tomlien in her face with her heel and heading for the door.

Everyone panics. Most of the guests rush for the door with Valentina, but not us. I plant myself in front of the doorway along with Serghei and Bryn, refusing to let the witch escape.

Valentina raises her hand. A fire fills her palm, but before she can shoot it at us a jet of water splashes over the fire in her hand, quenching it.

Valentina turns around slowly. At the other end of the church stands Shioni. She is breathing heavily, glare focused on her elder.

"I challenge you to a witches' duel," Shioni says violently. "Will you accept, Valentina, or are you too cowardly?"

"You have been a thorn in my side ever since you emerged from the Pool, weak caster," Valentina replies nastily. "It is time I finally finished the coven that has given me so much grief."

Valentina swoops her hand up. Fire starts at her feet, blazing throughout the room in a circle, like an explosion. Everyone except for Shioni dives to the floor, covering their head with their hands and pressing against the safety of the wall.

Shioni doesn't flinch, merely swings both arms upward like a wave. Water appears, picking up the pews and throwing them at Valentina.

Valentina isn't fazed. She creates a wall of fire around her, one that burns the pews to ashes the minute they touch her magic. She puts two index fingers together and shoots a column of fire at Shioni.

The young witch brings her hands inward, palms touching as if in a gesture of prayer. Water circles itself around Shioni's flame, circling her until the column is put out.

Lidia stays as subdued as the rest of us, pressing herself against the wall. Her magic cannot hope to compete against the power of these two Head Witches. All she can do is hide and hope they don't notice her.

I catch Lisar's eyes across the hall, trapped in a corner with Tomlien. Both of us are desperate to get to each other, but we don't dare risk crossing between these foes.

There's nothing that vampires or werewolves can do to stop this. This is a war of witches. The only ones who can end it are those who began it.

Valentina changes tactics. She swoops her hands above her head in a giant circle. A windstorm sweeps up within the church, bringing with it a torrential rain from dark clouds that cluster against the ceiling. Shioni responds in kind, curling her fingers until thunder shakes the stone below her feet and lightning emerges from her very fingertips.

Shioni shoots bolts of lightning at Valentina while attempting to resist the windstorm. All her shots miss. Valentina laughs nastily every time Shioni doesn't strike.

Frustrated, Shioni lets out a scream. She begins dismantling stone monuments from around the church and tosses them at Valentina. The old witch avoids them, as if bored.

When Shioni is worn out, Valentina points her hand above her head. The clouds filter downward, turning into a thick smoke. Shioni crosses herself with a protective spell hastily, but it doesn't work. The smoke filters into her mouth, ramming down her throat.

Shioni grasps at her neck. She begins twisting, falling to her knees and gasping for breath as Valentina snickers.

My hope begins to die as Shioni's skin starts to turn blue. This is it. There's no way out of this one.

Shioni is going to die. Just when I think this is the end, Shioni's throat utters a parched spell. Light begins beaming from her eyes, mouth, and ears. I have to shield my gaze from the brightness.

When I'm able to open my eyes again I see Valentina agape, Shioni standing on her feet triumphantly. I don't know what she did. All I know is Valentina's smoke is gone.

Valentina gives an angry cry. She starts firing random spells at Shioni, red, black and purple. Shioni returns with sparks of her own, her spells green and blue. Most miss, but some hit; Shioni starts foaming at the mouth... Valentina erupts into seizures before righting herself again... Shioni starts bleeding rapidly from a dark cut on her arm, which she heals... Valentina ceases the spreading of a dark spell that leaks through her veins.

While they're dueling, my eye catches someone moving across the room... Lidia, attempting to take Shioni from behind.

That's not going to happen. I hear Lisar crying out for me as I get up and start running through the spellfire.

"Lyssy, what are you doing?" he screams. I ignore his screams and keep my head down as I dash across the church.

Lidia sees me coming and casts a defensive spell, but even when it hits me and pain shatters across my body I don't do anything but grit my teeth and keep going. Lidia attempts to scramble out of the way, but my arms are around her and I've got her pinned to the floor before she can run.

While I've got her restrained, Valentina is distracted. It gives Shioni the few critical seconds she needs.

"*Mortis!*" Shioni cries. A black spell dashes from her hands, and its tendrils loop around Valentina, squeezing her body tightly.

Valentina attempts to cast spells. When that doesn't work, she tries to claw her way out of the cage, but the dark spell loops around her body like inky vines. The spell is full of thorns that pierce her body and sink in like daggers. Valentina emits a horrendous scream, apparently in unimaginable pain, but Shioni does not call off her spell. She merely squeezes her open hands into fists, driving the thorns in deeper.

The blood and muscle drain from Valentina's face until it appears she's nothing but skin stretched over a skeleton. Her eyes pop out of their sockets. They roll down her face and onto the floor as the skin burns away and the bones blacken.

Valentina gives a final yell of protest and agony before Shioni nods her head. Valentina turns into a pile of dust, never to be seen again.

I'm brought back to reality when I feel Lidia squirming underneath me. Her face is full of fear, eyes pleading as she gazes up at me, begging for mercy.

"Lysandra, I didn't mean anything I did to you," she flounders. "I was just jealous, I promise. Please, let me go!"

"You tried to kill Lisar," I snarl, retracting my fangs. "For that, nothing can be forgiven."

Lidia screams as I bend my head downward and sink my fangs into her neck. She claws at my eyes, attempting to get away, but I dig my fingers into her belly, pierce through the skin and pull to silence her weak attempts to free herself. Lidia's entrails slide against my hands as they fall out onto the floor. She goes limp, her heartbeat fading as I continue to drink from her veins like a rabid animal.

I only intend to take enough to kill her, but she's long since dead and I can't stop drinking. Human blood is the best thing I've ever tasted. It slips across my tongue, warm and salty, a precious gift of life like I've never had before. Something to savor. Human blood has got something different in it, an essence missing from every other creature. It's delicious... mind blowing... addictive.

I feel hands around my arms. They're trying to drag me away. I lash out, growling like a beast. Although I kick and scream, I'm not strong enough to pull away from those who have captured me. I struggle as the world comes back into focus, slowly regaining my mind...

"Lyssy." Lisar's hands are upon my face. His thumbs stroke my cheeks as he calms me down. "Hey. Lyssy, look at me, right at me. It's all right. Chill out."

I take deep, steadying breaths. As the room comes back into focus and stops being a raging blur, I see that those left in the room stare at me as if I'm a raging demon meant to be caged. I look at the hands firmly gripping my arms and see that it took both Lisar and Serghei to drag me off. Lidia's blood is all over my mouth, and my clothes. I stare down at her body, shocked by the sight of her organs on the ground, overwhelmed by the smell of her body permeating the room.

I did that. I killed Lidia in a violent way and drank her blood, even though I didn't need to.

I murdered my best friend. It's done.

TWENTY-THREE

*L*isar brings me back. The room comes into focus, and I look around the chapel. The pews are broken, flowers strewn about and decorations in disarray. Lisar's tux is torn, along with everyone's elses clothes. Lidia's blood soaks my dress. A disaster.

Serghei waves his hand. A few Salkovians come and take Lidia's body away, and sweep up the ashes Valentina left behind.

I am glad. I am happy to be rid of them.

There' something new underneath my regular hunger. My body is occupied by a sensation that has never come over it before. It is a desire that obsesses my deepest thoughts, a need that draws my attention even though all I can focus on is Lisar's face. My skin itches as if crawling with a thousand spiders. I scratch at my arms absentmindedly, throat parched. My entire body quakes with the want. Even now, I crave it.

I thirst for human blood.

Lisar slowly drops his hands from my face and embraces me instead. His hand rubs my back in slow circles as he says, "I'm sorry, Lyssy. I should've known it wasn't you."

"There was no way you could've," I whisper back. I pull away from him, and turn to Serghei. I need answers.

"Will it happen?" I ask him. "Will I become a Cursed One?"

Serghei's face is stern, but only to hide the sadness beneath. "You would have to drink more than one human's blood worth to turn. Though now the taste will always be there; you will never be able to rid yourself of it. Always you will long for the taste of human blood."

My insides churn. I have become the very thing I despised more than anything else. An addict.

I despise myself.

Bryn and Tomlien are holding onto each other. Tomlien kisses and and strokes Bryn's hair as she cries tears of relief into his chest. The curse has been lifted. They can finally be together again.

"Well, looks like that's over with," Bryn says, wiping her face and peeling away from Tom's grasp when she's finally done crying. "Thank Fane."

"BRYN!" five people shout at once. Now that the immediate threat is gone, everyone's suddenly remembered that Bryn is still alive.

Lisar gets to her first, tackling her to the ground and hugging her tightly. The rest of the wolves pile on top of her as if they were still animals, letting out cheers.

"Get off of me, you big lummox!" Bryn says, trying to push her brother away.

"How did you survive?" Lisar says, refusing to let her go. "It's a miracle!"

"Valentina found me, cured me, and tried to use me against you guys, but she couldn't enchant me because of the curse so she kept me prisoner in this enchanted castle until she kidnapped Lysandra and we escaped together." Bryn hurriedly explains the story as quickly as she can, swimming her way to the surface of the group hug.

"An enchanted castle?" Shioni speaks up for the first time since the battle. She appears tired, but still strong. I remind myself not to annoy her anytime soon. She's a force to be reckoned with. "What kind of castle?"

"It was very odd," I sub in. "The staircases and doors kept moving. I believe it was in France."

"That is Le Château De Mirr." Shioni raises an eyebrow. "Tell me, did you encounter a strange mirror there, one that may have had transporting abilities?"

"Yes. We used it to get home." Bryn finally caves in and gives firm hugs to each of the pack members before adding, "It was the only way."

"That is the same relic Valentina stole from my coven," Shioni says. She smiles slightly. "I'm glad to know that it'll soon be back in my possession again."

"Shioni, you saved all of us," Bryn says, fumbling her way out of the pile. She grabs her maidservant's arms. "If it wasn't for you we all would've died. You beat her. You defeated Valentina."

"I may have gained the upper hand against Valentina in battle, but I got lucky. I still failed all of you." Shioni's head hangs. "I cannot break the curse upon the wolves. The pack is stuck this way."

"Not necessarily," a familiar, croaking voice echoes from the back of the chapel. We all turn to see someone rise from the back pew, the only one left standing. She has the red cloak I've known to associate with witches, but when she throws her hood back, shock quakes through my body.

"Baba Yaga!" I gasp.

"*That's* Baba Yaga?" Georgie peeps. "She looks like my grandma."

Kipcha smacks Georgie on the back of the head. Everyone is at attention. Baba Yaga smiles and says, "Yes, my child, it is me."

"Baba Yaga, welcome," Shioni breathes, giving a curtsy. "I beg your pardon, but what are you doing here? You are a very long way from your forest."

"The vampire princess spoke words that resonated true to me," Baba Yaga responds. "I do not believe I should interfere in this war, but after some debating with myself, I decided there is no reason why I cannot revert things back to the way they should be."

"Wait. Are you saying..." Lisar says.

Baba Yaga raises her hands. From them glows a green, fierce magic, one that stems from her fingertips and drifts throughout the room. The tendrils wrap like fingers around Lisar, Kipcha, Rosa, and

Georgie, raising them into the air so they hover above all of us and float to the ceiling.

"Hey, I feel funny! Put me down!" Georgie protests.

"It's all right, Georgie," Kipcha tells him, grinning broadly. "Something's happening."

Rosa lets out a yelp, but it's not human-like. It's a bark. Unexpectedly, she explodes in mid-air back into a she-wolf, four paws and all.

"I'm back! I'm free!" Rosa cheers. The tendrils put her down and she starts running around the room in circles, yipping.

Georgie is next to change. He squirms in mid-air, but the moment he transforms his tail starts wagging. The little wolf does a dance when he touches back on the ground, bouncing around Fyor and barking for attention. Fyor smiles and pats Georgie on the head, which makes Rosa roll her eyes. Kipcha lets out a laugh as the big red wolf when he changes, which makes Elizaveta's eyes go wide.

I'm hardly paying attention to any of this. My eyes are too focused on Lisar.

When Lisar transforms, golden light wraps around him. Soon the sight of my sandy Alpha, a creature I believed I would never see again, appears. Lisar touches down lightly on all fours, appearing even larger and stronger than he once did.

He's beautiful. Untamed. Free.

"By Fane, we're back!" Lisar throws his head backwards and emits a howl that makes a shiver run down my spine. The rest of the wolves cry out with him, their howls shaking the very heavens. Bryn changes to join in. The pack is once again reunited, as they should be.

"Thank you, Baba Yaga," Lisar says when the howls end. He gives a wolfish bow to her, which the other wolves copy. "We can't thank you enough for this."

"I was merely restoring the balance, young Alpha." Baba Yaga sits back down in the pew. "You don't have to thank me."

"I seriously never want to change back ever again," Georgie says happily, wiggling his butt. "I'm staying like this forever."

"Hot damn, you people sure do know how to throw a wedding!" Kipcha says happily. "Best party ever!"

"What wedding?" I say. "Everything's ruined."

Lisar looks at me. I'm stunned to watch him change back already, reaching out as a human and taking my hands in his own.

"I don't think it is," Lisar says hopefully. "I'm still willing to go on ahead with this tonight. That is, if you want to."

"Of course I do. But how?" I ask desperately. "We have nothing."

"That's not true. The food is still good, and the band is ready to play the reception," Elizaveta offers. "Lisar is right. We shouldn't' let the party go to waste."

"Are you certain you want to host a wedding after such a gruesome battle?" Serghei asks dryly, gesturing to the chaos. "Lysandra has been through enough tonight. It's hardly the time."

"It's all right, Grandfather," I tell him. "I want this." I drop my head and sigh. "It could be a way to get my mind off all the sorrow."

"There couldn't be a more perfect time," Lisar argues before looking at me. "I promised to marry you today, and if you're all for it that's what I'm going to do."

"But… we don't have anything to wear," I say. "Or a place to hold the ceremony. We certainly can't hold it here in the chapel. It's ruined."

Elizaveta raises a finger. "I might have an answer for that."

TWENTY-FOUR

a few hours later, after I've gotten in a nap, taken a shower and consumed something that isn't human blood, I step into a dress made of white silk within the parlor room at the House of Antov.

My hair has been fashioned into a low bun, blush dotted across my pale cheeks, a soft pink rouge painted upon my lips. The dress has long sleeves, a drop waist and a flared skirt, an overlay of lace covering the satin. Pearl earrings hang from my lobes, and a long, golden necklace hangs a teardrop pearl down the center of my chest. White leather boots, tiny buttons lining the middle, finish the outfit.

"This is what Demetrius Dracula and Princess Anastasia wore at their wedding nearly a hundred years ago," Elizaveta told Lisar and I earlier, pressing the boxes into our hands. "We here at Salkovia were entrusted with them, but I think the situation warrants their use again."

Now I stand here appearing a bride straight out of the 1920s. In the hallway Serghei presses a silver crown onto my hair, topped with a white veil that ends at my knees.

"Your grandmother wore this at our wedding," he says gruffly. "I took it from Castel de Sange before I left, in hopes that we'd meet again and I'd get to see you wear it."

173

"Are you ready, Serghei?" I ask as he lifts the veil and places it gently over my face.

"I wasn't ready for this moment with your mother. But I am utterly convinced that this time will be different."

I smile at him. Around me, the other girls bustle around in their bridesmaid dresses, ready to march down the aisle. I can hear the classical music of the hardy band as they begin playing. One by one, the girls step out to walk.

"Hurry," Rosa says before she goes, still a wolf. She's the only one who refused to change back for the event, along with Georgie. "We only have a few more hours. The day is coming soon."

She slips out. Bryn is the last to walk. She gives me an encouraging wink before walking out with her bouquet.

I clutch mine tightly, a bouqet hastily made from the remnants of the flowers that weren't smashed in the chapel. For some strange reason, I don't feel nervous. Only at peace, like this is what I'm meant to do.

Serghei holds out his arm. "I will be with you every step of the way. Always, Granddaughter, will I be by your side."

I grasp Serghei's arm and take a deep breath. "Yes, Grandfather. I know."

The doors of the House of Antov open, unveiling the open courtyard lit by the light of the moon. The chairs have been arranged in a circle instead of a square, the altar replaced by a fountain. Soft snowflakes drift from the dark skies above, littered with stars. Red rose petals dropped by the bridesmaids decorate the path.

Waiting for me is Lisar. He wears a traditional navy blue hussar uniform, decorated with yellow buttons and red sleeve caps, golden tassels adorning the shoulders with navy pants tucked into high rise black leather boots. He looks all the part a prince.

If I had a heart, it would be pounding. Each step toward Lisar only seems to bring us farther away, but before I know it, I'm right beside him.

I'm shocked to see my Alpha's eyes sparkle with tears. What is he crying for? Am I really that pretty?

"Who gives the bride away?" Elizaveta asks, standing between us. As the leader of Salkovia, she is officiating the ceremony.

"I do," Serghei replies. He puts my hand in Lisar's, clamps his own firmly over ours, then steps back.

Elizaveta raises her hands. "Today we witness history. Never before has there been a union between a werewolf and a vampire. But the adoration these two have for each other proves that love has no boundaries. Love is blind. It experiences no prejudices, no hate, no assumptions. The bond that these two have formed cannot be expressed in words, but it can be summed up in the simple notion that these lovers chose to spare each other, *chose* to understand and look past what they had been told, despite all odds that were against them. When hatred was preached, they chose kindness. Where there was deceit, they chose trust. Where lies and rumors were spread, they chose to learn from one another and understand one another's truths. And when death came, they chose love. That love is what will heal our world today."

I get the feeling the rest of the guests already heard this the first time around, but it's special to me. Lisar's eyes gleam as they never have before. This is a truly magical moment, like something out of a fairy tale. Can this truly be happening to me? It's impossible, isn't it, for me to be this happy?

Elizaveta looks at Lisar. "Alpha Lisar Lepescu, do you hereby take Csarina Lysandra Katya Romanova-Dracula as your lawfully wedded wife, to have and to hold, to love and to cherish, in sickness and in health, as long as you both shall live?"

"Hell yes," Lisar says, smiling dashingly. I blush.

Elizaveta looks at me. "And do you, csarnia, take Alpha Lisar Lepescu to be your lawfully wedded husband, to have and to hold, to love and to cherish, in sickness and in health, as long as you both shall live?"

"Always," I respond quietly. "Forevermore."

"Do you have the ring?" Elizaveta asks Lisar. He nods. He takes my hand, and in place of the garnet engagement ring slips on a sparkling platinum ring decorated with hundreds of small diamonds, a large center stone in the middle that's larger than my fingernail. It takes my breath away just looking at it. Where in the world did Lisar get such a thing?

"If anyone objects to this union, speak now, or forever hold your peace."

Elizaveta nervously shifts at this part. Nobody dares to make a sound. I swear, if anyone objects right now I'm going to rip their head off. We've come too far to have our love challenged any longer.

When no one does, Elizaveta smiles and says, "Then by the power invested in me, I now pronounce you husband and wife. Lisar, you may kiss your bride."

Lisar puts a hand on the back of my neck and draws me forward, planting my lips on his. Quiet applause from the vampires sounds in the background, while obnoxious cheering screams from the wolves.

But I don't hear it. I'm too invested in Lisar's touch, lost in the revel of his soft lips caressing mine. This kiss, though so familiar, is different from all the rest. It's our first kiss as husband and wife, and everything has changed. We're not the same as we were before, and neither is our relationship. We've joined our souls together now in eternity. He is mine, and I am his. This is a testimony to our love, our way to show the world that no matter what, we're not separating. We're staying together and fighting for this, because it's the best thing we've ever known. Maybe even the only thing worth knowing in this cruel world.

The reception afterward is filled with joy. The ballroom in the House of Antov is decorated with beautiful Christmas garlands, hundreds of crystals hanging suspended from the ceilings like icicles. The tables have been outfitted with red velvet cloths, decorated with golden candelabras. The scene looks eerily similar to an Imperial Russian ball.

The guests cheer when Lisar and I enter. The band strikes up a soulful tune, a cello leading the way. Lisar places his hands on my waist. I place mine on his shoulders. We begin to sway back and forth with the music. Even though the whole room is watching us, I'm unable to take my eyes off Lisar.

"Would you have ever thought that our first dance back at Castel de Sange would've led us here?" Lisar asks softly.

"Never." I shake my head. Two tears slip out of my eyes. "I didn't think life could be this perfect."

"Hey, you've cried too much already," Lisar says, wiping the tears away. "Don't cry today. I'm yours, blondie. Always have been. Always will be."

I kiss him sweetly. This is the happiest I've ever been in my life. Perhaps the happiest I will ever be. If this is the pinnacle of joy in my life, I would be content, but I sense there are far greater joys to come.

I promised Lisar I wouldn't cry again, but I can't help it when it's Serghei and I's turn to waltz. Grandfather holds me stiffly and regally, the way a vampire should, though his normally stern face is tender and kind.

"Thank you for supporting me, Grandfather," I whisper to him as we end the dance. I embrace him tightly, and his whiskers scratch at my chin. "You stood by my side and accepted my love for Lisar when no one else in our family would."

"This seems so unreal to me." He sighs. "I can remember when you were placed in my arms as a small babe. Now you're a bride."

"You're no less important to me." I bite my lip as I pull away, to keep from spilling more tears. "Lisar is my husband now, but you have always been and will always be one of the most important people in my life."

"I will always protect you, Granddaughter. Your happiness is my happiness," he says. "I swore the moment you were born to safeguard you always. This will be so until the day that I die."

"Then let it never come." I kiss his cheek, and we part. As Serghei and I exit the dance floor, the fur-clothed Salkovians take our place to perform a Russian folk dance.

Georgie, in his wolf form, jumps up in the air to catch the bouquet, but when he sees Fyor looking at him he yelps. It ends up tumbling out of his mouth and falling into Bryn's hands instead.

She blushes. Tomlien gives her a devilish smile, the first I've ever seen from him. He ends up dragging her out of the reception hall, his arms wrapped around her torso and their mouths glued together.

"I can guess where they're headed!" Kipcha barks, and the party laughs. The band strikes up a quick song and Kipcha grabs Elizaveta around the waist, and sweeps her throughout the room. Flabbergasted, Elizaveta does nothing but allow herself to be waltzed clumsily around the ballroom by the beta. I can tell by the look on her face she enjoys being held in Kipcha's strong arms.

Rosa and Valeri throw food at each other and mumble under their breath about how much they hate the other. I suppose it's their way of getting along.

Towards the end of the reception Kipcha, Georgie, Rosa, and Bryn (who came back with her hair quite a mess) kidnap me, drag me up to an abandoned room and hold me for ransom, as is Romanian tradition. Lisar charges into the room bellowing, causing a ruckus. We end up tumbling into one another and falling into a giant heap, me with my veil knocked askew and the rest of them laughing at me for it.

A well of affection rises in my chest for these people. Here, surrounded by dear friends and finally wedded to my true love, a tender thought crosses my mind. This wedding isn't just a wedding. It's the first step toward forever.

TWENTY-FIVE

"I seriously cannot wait to get to Italy," Lisar says in our bedroom, flipping over the lid of the suitcase and lying on top of it in order to zip it up. He struggles with the zipper as he says, "It'll be amazing to get a vacation."

"I agree with you," I say, smiling. Ever since the wedding Lisar has been so excited to catch a break. His happiness is my happiness.

My arms itch again and I scratch at them quickly, though it's not going to help. My throat feels as dry as a bone, despite drinking four bottles of blood that morning. I'm so thirsty.

I thought my desire to consume human blood would fade with time. Not true. The craving is just as strong, if not stronger than it was when it first entered my body. It makes me nervous to be vacationing in a place where there are so many humans, instead of staying here where there's only vampires and werewolves.

But I reason that I have to get over this eventually and learn to control it, so Lisar and I made plans for Verona and I crushed down the feelings of anxiety that came with it.

Baba Yaga stayed with us for a few days after the wedding before returning home. She told me before she left that I wouldn't see her again. Beyond returning the wolves to their formal state, she wanted no more part in this war.

I didn't argue. She'd done enough.

"Do you think they can handle everything while we're gone?" I ask nervously. It takes all my self-control for me not to scratch myself again.

"Elizaveta and Kipcha have got it covered. It's only two weeks," Lisar says firmly. "Lyssy, why are you so worried? We talked about this. Everything's gonna be fine."

"I've just been feeling a little… funny lately," I respond. And it's true. I have been feeling off, and it's not because of the addiction. Something about my body isn't right. I haven't been sick, per say, just different. I don't know what's wrong, and I don't like it.

Lisar cups my chin. "You'll be fine once we get out of here. I really think you just need to relax for a few days. It's our honeymoon! Cheer up."

He kisses me on the cheek. I giggle and say, "You acted like the honeymoon started the night of the wedding. You haven't left me alone since."

"And you can bet that's going to continue. You won't be able to walk when we get home," Lisar responds. He lugs the suitcase off the bed and starts dragging it down the hallway.

I putter around the room, picking up various things and putting them in order, making sure we packed everything. But it's not because I need to. Really, I'm stalling. I want to go to Italy. At the same time, I don't want to leave Salkovia. Something about going away seems dangerous.

The door creaks, and a sour smell infects the room. I turn around. I expect it's Lisar returning, but it's not.

It's Ivan Grigory.

He looks the same, every bit the person he was in my nightmares. Long, clawed fingernails reach down to his knees, ready to strike. A convoluted face. A thick nose, and sickly white skin.

"No," I whisper, thinking I'm hallucinating. My knees quake. "This isn't real. You're dead. Lisar killed you."

Ivan grins. His rotting fangs poke from between his chapped lips. "Surprise, pretty girl. Dragomir's witch saved me. I came by as a personal thank you that you killed her. She had her hold on me for quite some time. I was tired of doing her dirty work."

"What do you want with me?" I ask. I fumble around the coffee table for my knife, and hold it aloft. Ivan smirks at my blade as if we're playing a game.

"There's a war coming, don't you see? All the bodies and blood we can drink. Your daddy promised me and my followers land in Romania if we delivered you to him." Ivan crouches down. "He made me swear alive, though I think he won't mind if you come back a little… dead."

Ivan springs. I scream, and bring the knife slashing upward.

It misses, and Ivan sails over me. He snarls as he hits the wall, stunned. As he turns his hellish eyes on me once more, I scream again.

It doesn't take but a few seconds for Lisar to come bolting in. He's flanked by Bryn and Tom, both at the ready. Lisar changes into a wolf and charges at Ivan, snarling. Bryn follows his lead and the two wolves pin him against the wall. They deliver crushing bites as Ivan howls in pain.

Tom stoops down to my side. "Lysandra, are you okay?" he asks, placing a hand on my shoulder.

I cannot reply. I'm shaking all over.

Clumsily, Ivan grabs Bryn by the scruff of the neck and tosses her across the room. She fumbles over the bed, while Ivan delivers a harsh kick to Lisar. My wolf groans as Ivan's foot hits him straight in the gut, winding him.

"I'm coming for you, princess! Wait and see!" Ivan's maniacal cackles can be heard as he breaks the window with his nails. He clambers through the broken glass and runs for dear life to the outside world.

"Don't let him escape!" Lisar screams. "Stop him!"

Bryn hops out through the window to give chase while Tomlien leaves to alert the other vampires. Soon, alarm bells are ringing all throughout Salkovia. *Ding, ding, ding.* They rattle in my ears, my head, through my organs.

They are inescapable. Just like my fate.

"Lyssy." Lisar is a man again. He stoops downward, picks me up in his arms and cradles me against his chest, rocking me back and forth. "Are you okay?"

I nod, just to make him think I am. But despite the warrior face I put on for my beloved Alpha, I'm forced to admit to myself I'm not okay.

I'm really not.

* * *

I DIDN'T HAVE to be told that Ivan Grigory got away.

All of Salkovia has been turned upside down trying to locate him, but I doubt they will. He wouldn't have come at me so boldly tonight if he didn't have an escape plan. Elizaveta posts guards around me, to defend me at all times, but I know how to get away from them.

I don't want anyone tailing me right now.

While Lisar is preoccupied with trying to find Ivan, I slip away and run off to Shioni's chambers. The answer of what's wrong with me became so clear when Ivan attacked, like instinct. I only need someone to confirm it.

Shioni is working on a potion when I enter the room. The mirror, the one Bryn and I used to get back to Salkovia, is propped up against the wall. Shioni went to France and obtained it the moment the wedding was over. I'm glad she has it back again, though it worries me such a powerful object is in her possession. If our enemies discover it's here, they will want to claim it.

"Lysandra," she says in surprise. "I thought you were under lock-down. You shouldn't be wandering around the house by yourself."

"Never mind that," I say quickly. "What are you brewing?"

"A finding spell for locating Grigory. I assure you we're all working very hard to catch him." Shioni starts stirring the potion. It eats away at her wooden spoon. I'm not sure she's made it right.

"Don't work too hard, Shioni. He's already gone." I sit down on a chair in her room. Suddenly, I've become winded and lightheaded.

Shioni glances upward. "I figured as much. But why are you here?"

I sit upright. "It's become clear to me the witches need a kingdom of their own. As csarina, I only think it right that you should lead them."

"Me?" Shioni stops stirring the pot and stumbles backwards in surprise. "Why?"

"You defeated Valentina. After this war is over if you want to return to Le Château De Mirr and rule from there, I would support you. You are a powerful witch... a queen of witches, if I may suggest it. Help us win and I'll live up to my promise to put you on the throne."

Shioni nods. "This is a great honor. If you truly believe in me this much, I'll accept."

Then she hesitates. "Though this isn't the reason you came to me tonight. Is it?"

I shake my head. "No. I... I need answers." I swallow down a pit of nervousness. I get up from my chair and venture to her side. "And you have them. Don't you, Shioni?"

She's pointedly avoiding my eyes. "You don't want to know."

I reach out to grab her wrist. "Shioni, you know. Tell me the truth."

* * *

AN HOUR later I'm sitting on the edge of the fountain in the greenhouse sobbing, which seems like the place to go when you're emotionally distraught. I've went through an entire box of tissues and am starting on my second. I seriously can't stop crying.

What am I going to say to Lisar? What am I going to say to *anyone*?

"Lysandra?" Serghei's booming voice echoes throughout the greenhouse. It only makes me cringe, and cry harder.

He comes around the corner. His stone visage becomes concerned when he notices the tears trickling down my cheeks.

"Granddaughter, what is wrong?" he asks, sitting next to me on the fountain. He puts an arm around me and pulls me to his side gently. "I know we didn't catch Ivan, but we will. You have nothing to fear."

"It isn't that," I sniffle. You can barely understand me through the tears. I'm such a mess right now. "Oh, Grandfather, everything is just awful!"

"There now." Serghei takes a handkerchief from his coat pocket. He dabs it at the tears falling from my eyes, grabs my hand and says, "Tell me everything."

* * *

THE THIN DAWN blooms on the Siberian tundra's horizon.

My legs are curled up, arms wrapped around them, the side of my head on my knees as I sit upon the roof of the House of Antov. I want to watch the sun rise before it gets too light and I have to go inside.

Strange. I feared the sun so much before.

It doesn't make me feel anything now.

The door behind me, the one that goes to the attic, creaks open. I don't move to see who it is. I can smell my lover's sweet scent drifting through my hair.

"Lyssy, where have you been?" Lisar's tone is originally panicked and angry, though it changes to worried when he joins my side. "We've been looking for you for hours."

"I've been up here," I mumble. Lisar sits beside me, crossing his legs. His eyes look utterly confused, and somewhat disturbed.

"Lyssy, are you…"

He shakes his head. He knows better than to ask if I'm all right. "What do I need to do?"

"Just sit with me," I say quietly. "Please."

"Okay." Lisar sits beside me. He doesn't say anything, and neither do I as the sun blossoms over the earth. We only have minutes now before the shadows break and it will no longer be safe for me to be outside. Still, I try to preserve the moment as long as I can. I want to watch the sunrise up until the last minute, when the treasure slips away.

After a time, Lisar breaks the silence.

"It's a beautiful sight, isn't it?" Lisar says. "Salkovia. I never really noticed before."

"Yes. I suppose it is." I squeeze my knees tighter to my body.

"We can't go to Italy now, can we?" Lisar asks solemnly.

"We can and we should," I say. "We need to."

"Is now really the best time for a vacation, babe?" Lisar asks doubtfully.

"Not for our honeymoon. For safety," I say. "We need to take the others and leave immediately. All the wolves. Serghei. Tomlien. Even Elizaveta, if she can spare leaving Slakovia to the council. Salkovia is fortified, but Dragomir knows we're here. It's not safe. We need to go into hiding for a few months, make a plan of action and then regroup."

"I've already contacted the other packs," Lisar says. "They expect to meet us here in Salkovia."

"Tell them that the plan has changed," I say. "They can meet up with us where we land."

I don't like this, giving orders to my beloved. But I am csarina, and I have a duty to protect the ones I love the most. Italy is the best option. Lisar will understand once I explain.

Lisar's eyes are still curious. "All right... mind if I ask why you're making all these sudden decisions?"

I can't buy any more time. I have to tell him.

"We can't keep doing this, Lisar," I say tiredly. "We can't avoid Dragomir anymore. It doesn't do any good. He always finds us."

"Maybe we haven't run far enough away yet."

I shake my head. "No. Serghei was right. There's no place we can hide, or can go. Dragomir won't stop hunting us until he has what he wants."

"Do you really think that's true?"

"Yes. We have to defeat Dragomir. It's either us or him. He's not gonna stop until he kills us. That's why we have to go to Italy. It'll buy us some time to make a plan."

I refuse to be dragged back to Castel de Sange. I'll take my own life before Dragomir takes mine. Being forced back into a life of servitude for that hideous monster, after I've tasted freedom, is a fate worse than death. I've been living away from him for a while now, but I'm not truly out of his grasp. I never have been. He's going to kill me.

Unless I kill him first.

"I know we beat Valentina, but that's a different story," Lisar argues. "Dragomir has an empire, and we're so tiny. If we go up against him he'll squash us."

"We have to try." I run a hand through my hair. "Ivan's presence here only means things are going to get worse. Dragomir sent him to mess with us. He's not going to play nice now that we've killed his most powerful pawn."

"Yeah. And if Ivan Grigory's running around with Dragomir I can almost bet Vasile's joined up with them, too," Lisar adds.

"An army of Cursed Ones and Haunted on Dragomir's side." I shake my head, and put my lips against my shoulder. "This is impossible."

"Nothing's impossible." Lisar rubs my back. "Not with us."

I waver back and forth at Lisar's touch. My conversation with Shioni this afternoon still has me rattled. The prophecy. I can't help Nicolae's words from rambling about in my head. They've been bothering me ever since I spoke with her.

"You will be the end of our race. Of my son. If you truly love him as you say, you'll let him go."

As evil as he was, I feel like he was right.

"I'm going to kill Dragomir. That's the end of it," I say abruptly. It sounds so ridiculous out loud, though it was confident in my head.

"Why?" Lisar asks. "A few months ago you didn't want anything to do with resisting Dragomir. Why do you want to fight him now?"

"Because we don't have a choice!" I shout. My lip quivers, and tears form in my eyes as I reach out to grasp him.

Panic resonates on his face, as well as shock. Joy. A combination of celebration and mourning darkens his brown eyes, masked by a state of fear. He knows what I'm going to say.

I take a steadying breath. It only makes me fall apart. "Lisar. I'm pregnant."

* * *

Lisar and Lysandra's romantic story comes to a shocking conclusion in the grand finale of *The Shifter Prophecy, Book Four: Heir to Russia.*

Like magic and dragon shifters? Receive a FREE copy of THE WITCH'S CURSE by signing up for Megan Linski's VIP list here!

Megan Linski can be found on www.meganlinski.com, her Facebook page, her Twitter Page, and on Goodreads.

If you liked this book, please leave a review on Goodreads, Amazon, or your online eBook retailer.

Check out Gryfyn Publishing on their website, Facebook, and Twitter.

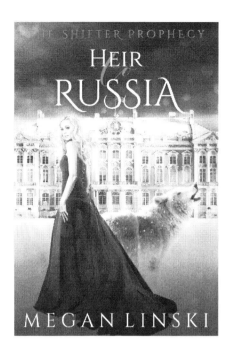

Heir to Russia
The Shifter Prophecy, Book #4

The future of the vampires— and the fate of the shifters— rests upon the shoulders of Russia's last heir.

The time for running is over. The time for war has just begun. As the only surviving member of the Romanov family save for Csar Dragomir, Lysandra is in a fight for survival. Her worst enemies are around every corner, hunting for a mystical item that will change the course of the war. Using clues left behind by her ancestor, Princess Anastasia, Lysandra must find it before they do... or suffer the horrors of the undead.

But even an artifact as powerful as the one they're searching for cannot compare to Lisar and Lysandra's greatest challenge. Before the lovers can see what's coming, tragedy strikes, and their romance will never be the same. The ending result will change their love story forever... and, potentially, end their marriage.

Friends fall. Death is rampant. Couples unite, and the meaning of true love is explored as Lysandra and her companions put everything on the line to bring down a tyrant whose madness knows no end. In the final conclusion of what began as the star crossed tale of a vampire princess and her wolf, who will make the ultimate sacrifice for love?

Family, friendship, and inner beauty are all part of the heart stopping finale of The Shifter Prophecy series. USA Today Bestselling Author Megan Linski's ending to a paranormal romance saga full of strong heroines, Alpha males, and magic will leave readers laughing and in tears during the final book of a young adult fantasy collection for this generation.

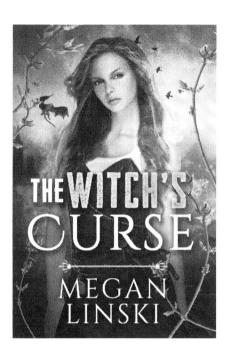

THE WITCH'S CURSE

"The scream of a dying girl was the singular sound that changed my life, forever."

When Briar enters the Eldermere Woods alone, she never could've imagined the danger that awaited her there. As a young witch, she's sought by hunters who desire her blood, a group of radicals who wish to eliminate all magical creatures. When Briar discovers a fellow witch slaughtered in the forest, her boring afternoon is changed into a fight for her life.

With the help of her dragon shifter love, Thomas, Briar must find a way to stop the witch hunters from destroying her town of Thorny Brook. But is her magic strong enough to defeat her most dangerous enemies? Full of danger, fantasy, and fun, *THE WITCH'S CURSE* is another thrilling installment by bestselling author Megan Linski.

Now FREE by signing up for Megan Linski's VIP list!

ACKNOWLEDGMENTS

War of Witches was a project that took a larger amount of research than its prequels. I would like to thank my editor, Thalia, for helping me to compile and organize this book, as well as suggesting scenes for me to add that, ultimately, made the book better.

I also would like to thank you, dear reader, for supporting my writing efforts by reading *War of Witches.* I hope that you're looking forward to devouring the series grand finale, *Heir to Russia.*

ABOUT THE AUTHOR

Megan Linski is the owner of Gryfyn Publishing and has had a passion for writing ever since she completed her first (short) novel at the age of 6. Her specializations are romance, fantasy, and contemporary fiction for young and new adults. When not writing she enjoys ice skating, horse riding, theatre, archery, fishing, and being outdoors. She is a passionate advocate for mental health awareness and suicide prevention, and is an active fighter against common variable immune deficiency disorder. She lives in Michigan.

www.meganlinski.com
gryfynpublishing@gmail.com

28282096R00118

Printed in Great Britain
by Amazon